THE GAME'S A

Now, match wits with the world's greatest consulting detective. And have no fear — if you don't completely succeed at first, just play again! It might be wise to keep in mind Holmes' advice to Watson and all would-be detectives:

> *"It is an old maxim of mine," he said, "that when you have eliminated the impossible, whatever remains, however improbable, must be the truth."*

SHERLOCK HOLMES SOLO MYSTERIES™ — developed by Iron Crown Enterprises — present a series of living mystery novels designed for solitary game play. In each gamebook, the reader is the detective who must solve or prevent a crime — with Sherlock Holmes and Dr. Watson as allies.

**Look for a new gamebook in the
SHERLOCK HOLMES SOLO
MYSTERIES™ series every other month
from Berkley and Iron Crown Enterprises!**

Cover Design: Richard H. Britton

System Editor: S. Coleman Charlton

Production: Suzanne Young, Richard H. Britton, Kurt
   Fischer, Jessica Ney, John Ruemmler, Paula Peters,
   Larry Brook, Leo LaDell, Eileen Smith

SHERLOCK HOLMES
SOLO MYSTERIES™

THE HONOUR OF THE YORKSHIRE LIGHT ARTILLERY

by Gerald Lientz

Content Editor: John David Ruemmler
Managing Editor: Kevin Barrett
Cover Art by Daniel Horne
Illustrations by Bob Versandi

CHARACTER RECORD

Name: JAMES G. HURLEY

Skill	Bonus	Equipment:
Athletics	+1	1) PENCIL
Artifice	+1	2) PAPER
Observation	+1	3) POCKET KNIFE
Intuition	+1	4) SKELETON KEYS
Communication	+1	5)
Scholarship	+1	6)
		7)

Money:		
____ pence	8)
10 shillings	9)
____ guineas	10)
3 pounds	11)

NOTES:

CHARACTER RECORD

Name:

Skill	Bonus	Equipment:
Athletics	_____	1)
Artifice	_____	2)
Observation	_____	3)
Intuition	_____	4)
Communication	_____	5)
Scholarship	_____	6)
		7)

Money: _____pence | 8)

_____shillings | 9)

_____guineas | 10)

_____pounds | 11)

NOTES:

CLUE SHEET

- ☐ A _____
- ☐ B _____
- ☐ C _____
- ☐ D _____
- ☐ E _____
- ☐ F _____
- ☐ G _____
- ☐ H _____
- ☐ I _____
- ☐ J _____
- ☐ K _____
- ☐ L _____
- ☐ M _____
- ☐ N _____
- ☐ O _____
- ☐ P _____
- ☐ Q _____
- ☐ R _____
- ☐ S _____
- ☐ T _____
- ☐ U _____
- ☐ V _____
- ☐ W _____
- ☐ X _____
- ☐ Y _____
- ☐ Z _____
- ☐ AA _____
- ☐ BB _____
- ☐ CC _____
- ☐ DD _____
- ☐ EE _____
- ☐ FF _____

DECISIONS & DEDUCTIONS SHEET

- ☐ 1 _____
- ☐ 2 _____
- ☐ 3 _____
- ☐ 4 _____
- ☐ 5 _____
- ☐ 6 _____
- ☐ 7 _____
- ☐ 8 _____
- ☐ 9 _____
- ☐ 10 _____
- ☐ 11 _____
- ☐ 12 _____
- ☐ 13 _____
- ☐ 14 _____
- ☐ 15 _____
- ☐ 16 _____
- ☐ 17 _____
- ☐ 18 _____
- ☐ 19 _____
- ☐ 20 _____
- ☐ 21 _____
- ☐ 22 _____
- ☐ 23 _____
- ☐ 24 _____
- ☐ 25 _____
- ☐ 26 _____

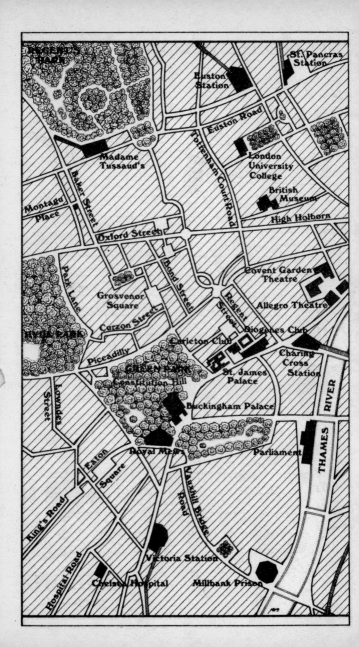

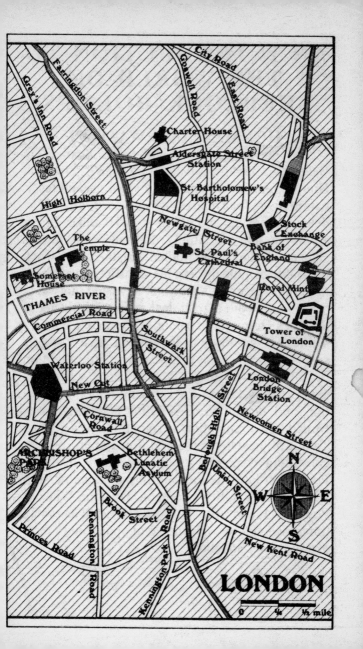

AN INTRODUCTION TO THE WORLD OF SHERLOCK HOLMES

HOLMES AND WATSON

First appearing in "A Study in Scarlet" in Beeton's Christmas Annual of 1887, Sherlock Holmes remains a remarkably vigorous and fascinating figure for a man of such advanced years. The detective's home and office at 221B Baker Street are shrines now, not simply rooms in which Holmes slept and deduced and fiddled with the violin when he could not quite discern the significance of a clue or put his finger on a criminal's twisted motive.

We know both a great deal and very little about Sherlock Holmes as a person. The son of a country squire (and grandson of the French artist Vernet's sister), Holmes seems to have drawn little attention to himself until his University days, where his extraordinary talents for applying logic, observation and deduction to solving petty mysteries earned him a reputation as something of a genius. Taking the next logical step, Holmes set up a private consulting detective service, probably in 1878. Four years later, he met and formed a partnership with a former military surgeon, Dr. John Watson. Four novels and fifty-six short stories tell us everything we know of the odd pair and their extraordinary adventures.

Less a well-rounded individual than a collection of contradictory and unusual traits, Holmes seldom exercised yet was a powerful man of exceptional speed of foot. He would eagerly work for days on a case with no rest and little food, yet in periods of idleness would refuse to get out of bed for days. Perhaps his most telling comment appears in "The Adventure of the Mazarin Stone:"

I am a brain, Watson. The rest of me is a mere appendix.

Holmes cared little for abstract knowledge, once noting that it mattered not to him if the earth circled the sun or vice versa. Yet he could identify scores of types of tobacco ash or perfume by sight and odor, respectively. Criminals and their modus operandi obsessed him; he pored over London's sensational newspapers religiously.

A master of disguise, the detective successfully presented himself as an aged Italian priest, a drunken groom, and even an old woman! A flabbergasted Watson is the perfect foil to Holmes, who seems to take special delight in astonishing his stuffy if kind cohort.

In "The Sign of Four," Holmes briefly noted the qualities any good detective should possess in abundance (if possible, intuitively): heightened powers of observation and deduction, and a broad range of precise (and often unusual) knowledge. In this *Sherlock Holmes Solo Mysteries*™ adventure, you will have ample opportunity to test yourself in these areas, and through replaying the adventure, to improve your detective skills.

Although impressive in talent and dedication to his profession, Sherlock Holmes was by no means perfect. Outfoxed by Irene Adler, Holmes readily acknowledged defeat by "the woman" in "A Scandal in Bohemia." In 1887, he admitted to Watson that three men had outwitted him (and Scotland Yard). The lesson Holmes himself drew from these failures was illuminating:

> *Perhaps when a man has special knowledge and special powers like my own, it rather encourages him to seek a complex explanation when a simpler one is at hand.*

So learn to trust your own observations and deductions — when they make sense and match the physical evidence and the testimony of trusted individuals — don't rush to judgment, and if you like and the adventure allows, consult Holmes or Watson for advice and assistance.

VICTORIAN LONDON

When Holmes lived and worked in London, from the early 1880's until 1903, the Victorian Age was much more than a subject of study and amusement. Queen Victoria reigned over England for more than 60 years, an unheard of term of rule; her tastes and inhibitions mirrored and formed those of English society. Following the Industrial Revolution of roughly 1750-1850, England leaped and stumbled her way from a largely pastoral state into a powerful, flawed factory of a nation. (The novels of Charles Dickens dramatically depict this cruel, exhilarating period of sudden social change.) Abroad, imperialism planted the Union Jack (and implanted English mores) in Africa, India, and the Far East, including Afghanistan, where Dr. Watson served and was wounded.

Cosmopolitan and yet reserved, London in the late Nineteenth Century sported over six million inhabitants, many from all over the world; it boasted the high society of Park Lane yet harbored a seedy Chinatown where opium could be purchased and consumed like tea. To orient yourself, consult the two-page map of London found immediately preceding this introduction. You will see that Baker Street is located just south of Regent's Park, near the Zoological Gardens, in the heart of the stylish West End of the city. Railway and horse-drawn carriages were the preferred means of transport; people often walked, and thieves frequently ran to get from one place to another.

THE GAME'S AFOOT!

Now, match wits with the world's greatest consulting detective. And have no fear — if you don't completely succeed at first, just play again! It might be wise to keep in mind Holmes' advice to Watson and all would-be detectives:

"It is an old maxim of mine," he said, "that when you have eliminated the impossible, whatever remains, however improbable, must be the truth."

Good luck and good hunting!

THE *SHERLOCK HOLMES SOLO MYSTERIES*™ GAME SYSTEM

THE GAMEBOOK

This gamebook describes hazards, situations, and locations that may be encountered during your adventures. As you read the text sections, you will be given choices as to what actions you may take. What text section you read will depend on the directions in the text and whether the actions you attempt succeed or fail.

Text sections are labeled with three-digit numbers (e.g.,"365"). Read each text section only when told to do so by the text.

PICKING A NUMBER

Many times during your adventures in this game-book you will need to pick a number (between 2 and 12). There are several ways to do this:

1) Turn to the Random Number Table at the end of this book, use a pencil (or pen or similar object), close your eyes, and touch the Random Number Table with the pencil. The number touched is the number which you have picked. If your pencil falls on a line, just repeat the process. **or**

2) Flip to a random page in the book and look at the small boxed number in the inside, bottom corner of the page. This number is the number which you have picked. **or**

3) If you have two six-sided dice, roll them. The result is the number which you have picked. (You can also roll one six-sided die twice and add the results.)

Often you will be instructed to pick a number and add a "bonus". When this happens, treat results of more than 12 as "12" and treat results of less than 2 as "2".

INFORMATION, CLUES, AND SOLVING THE MYSTERY

During play you will discover certain clues (e.g., a footprint, murder weapon, a newspaper article) and make certain decisions and deductions (e.g., you decide to follow someone, you deduce that the butler did it). Often the text will instruct you to do one of the following:

Check Clue xx or *Check Decision xx* or *Check Deduction xx.*

"xx" is a letter for Clues and a number for Decisions and Deductions. When this occurs, check the appropriate box on the "Clue Record Sheets" found at the beginning of the book. You should also record the information gained and note the text section number on the line next to the box. You may copy or photocopy these sheets for your own use.

Other useful information not requiring a "check" will also be included in the text. You may want to take other notes, so a "NOTES" space is provided at the bottom of your "Character Record". Remember that some of the clues and information given may be meaningless or unimportant (i.e., red herrings).

EQUIPMENT AND MONEY

Whenever you acquire money and equipment, record them on your Character Record in the spaces provided. Pennies (1 Pence), shillings (12 pence), guineas (21 shillings), and pounds (20 shillings) are "money" and may be used during your adventures to pay for food, lodging, transport, bribes, etc. Certain equipment may affect your abilities as indicated by the text.

You begin the adventure with the money noted on the completed Character Record sheet near the front of the book.

CHOOSING A CHARACTER
There are two ways to choose a character:
1) You can use the completely created character provided at the beginning of the book. **or**
2) You can create your own character using the simple character development system included in the next section of this book.

STARTING TO PLAY
After reading the rules above and choosing a character to play, start your adventures by reading the Prologue found after the rules section. From this point on, read the passages as indicated by the text.

CREATING YOUR OWN CHARACTER
If you do not want to create your own character, use the pre-created character found in the front of this book. If you decide to create your own character, follow the directions given in this section. Keep track of your character on the blank Character Record found in the front of this book. It is advisable to enter information in pencil so that it can be erased and updated. If necessary, you may copy or photocopy this Character Record for your own use.

As you go through this character creation process, refer to the pre-created character in the front of the book as an example.

SKILLS

The following 6 "Skill Areas" affect your chances of accomplishing certain actions during your adventures.

1) **Athletics** (includes fitness, adroitness, fortitude, pugnacity, fisticuffs): This skill reflects your ability to perform actions and maneuvers requiring balance, coordination, speed, agility, and quickness. Such actions can include fighting, avoiding attacks, running, climbing, riding, swimming, etc.

2) **Artifice** (includes trickery, disguise, stealth, eavesdropping): Use this skill when trying to move without being seen or heard (i.e., sneaking), trying to steal something, picking a lock, escaping from bonds, disguising yourself, and many other similar activities.

3) **Intuition** (includes sensibility, insight, reasoning, deduction, luck): This skill reflects your ability to understand and correlate information, clues, etc. It also reflects your ability to make guesses and to have hunches.

4) **Communication** (includes interviewing, acting, mingling, negotiating, diplomacy): This skill reflects your ability to talk with, negotiate with, and gain information from people. It also reflects your "social graces" and social adaptivity, as well as your ability to act and to hide your own thoughts and feelings.

5) **Observation** (includes perception, alertness, empathy): This skill reflects how much information you gather through visual perception.

6) **Scholarship** (includes education, science, current events, languages): This skill reflects your training and aptitude with various studies and sciences: foreign languages, art, history, current events, chemistry, tobaccory, biology, etc.

SKILL BONUSES

For each of these skills, you will have a Skill Bonus that is used when you attempt certain actions. When the text instructs you to "add your bonus," it is referring to these Skill Bonuses. Keep in mind that these "bonuses" can be negative as well as positive.

When you start your character, you have six "+1 bonuses" to assign to your skills.

You may assign more than one "+1 bonuses" to a given skill, but no more than three to any one skill. Thus, two "+1 bonuses" assigned to a skill will be a "+2 bonus", and three "+1 bonuses" will be a "+3 bonus". Each of these bonuses should be recorded in the space next to the appropriate skill on your Character Record.

If you do not assign any "+1 bonuses" to a skill, you must record a "-2 bonus" in that space.

During play you may acquire equipment or injuries that may affect your bonuses. Record these modifications in the "Bonus" spaces.

Cast of Characters

Beach: butler at Eagle Towers

Dr. John Cunningham: guest and friend of Colonel Dunlop.

Colonel Alexander Dunlop: former commander of the Yorkshire Lights and owner of Eagle Towers.

Miss Ellen Dunlop: his niece, engaged to Robert Harris.

Hunter Foxx: son of an officer in the Yorkshire Lights, formerly engaged to Miss Susan Mortimer.

Thomas Grayson: solicitor, guest of the Colonel.

Robert Harris: fiance of Miss Dunlop.

James G. Hurley: cousin of Dr. Watson and hero ("You") of this book.

Lieutenant John Jackson: guest at Eagle Towers.

Captain Eric Leaf: former officer in the Yorkshire Lights.

Lieutenant John Mortimer: ex-officer, young country gentleman, brother of Susan Mortimer.

Susan Mortimer: engaged to Robert Snead.

Mr. and Mrs. Mortimer: parents of John and Susan.

Badger Phillips: poacher.

Redruth: groundskeeper at Eagle Towers.

Mrs. Reynolds: housekeeper at Eagle Towers.

Robert Snead: Canadian, great grandson of an officer in the Yorkshire Lights, engaged to Miss Mortimer.

You have a pencil, paper, a pocketknife, and 3 pounds and 10 shillings in cash. Enter these items on your Character Record. You may also choose one of the following items and add it to your Character Record: a walking stick, a set of skeleton keys, or a magnifying glass.

PROLOGUE

Recently the London newpapers have been filled with accounts of two jewel thefts at country manors in the west of England. You assume that your mentor Sherlock Holmes will be asked to investigate the thefts and long for the day when you will be entrusted with such important matters. To your delight, you receive a note from your cousin, Dr. Watson, inviting you to come to 221-B Baker Street, "...as you may be able to assist in a matter referred to Holmes."

On a pleasant and surprisingly dry summer day in 1890, you waste no time hurrying to their Baker Street residence. As Mrs. Hudson opens the door, she seems perturbed and distracted. "You had best hurry, young man; there's a trip in the offing. I've made sandwiches," she whispers conspiratorially. You run up the stairs two at a time.

Holmes and Watson greet you hastily. Inside the chilly, crowded room, your heart races to be so near the brilliant mind

you emulate. By the bags resting by the door to their sitting room, you note that at least one of them is prepared to take a trip. Before you can press your cousin for news of the thefts and your involvement in the investigation, the detective cuts you off.

"Well, which of us is travelling?" Holmes asks, a light of merriment in his eye. "Examine the bags and see if you can tell." You study the customs markings on the luggage. *Pick a number* and add your Scholarship bonus:

- *If 2-6, turn to 161.*
- *If 7-12, turn to 306.*

100

"Your niece has keys to the padlocks that secured the eagle," you say. "She knew that she could free it quickly — no other individual could be certain of that."

"Well, that piece of evidence points to her," Holmes admits. "Do you have other reasons to accuse her?" *Turn to 437.*

101

It is not easy to set the trap you have planned, although the metal plates and heavy vases in the library offer a wide variety of choice. With Watson's help, you manage to arrange them, almost dropping one of the plates as you set it up. *Pick a number and add your Artifice bonus.*
- *If 2-7, turn to 343.*
- *If 8-12, turn to 222.*

102

You had taken some time after breakfast yesterday to study a large map of the estate. Concentrating on your memory of it, you remember a path that will allow you to intercept Grayson, but you will have to run hard to catch him. Is it worth it?
- *If you return to the house, turn to 200.*
- *If you continue your pursuit, turn to 313.*

103

Amid the sounds of distress and anger of everyone at the duel, one voice overwhelms all others. Mr. Mortimer yells at Susan: "Even if someone else loaded the gun, Mr. Snead was supposed to aim wide."

Snead begins to defend himself, then stops. "Perhaps I had better leave," he says. "I will inform the Colonel and arrange to take the evening train to London." Miss Mortimer's tears cannot sway either her father or her fiance.

The only cool head seems to be that of Ellen Dunlop. As soon as the doctors complete their preliminary examination of Mortimer, she announces: "The rest of you shall wait here. I will go to the house, arrange for the servants to bring a cot to carry John, and prepare a room for him downstairs." Before anyone can suggest an alternative plan, she hurries to the house. Soon, several servants appear, carrying a cot and blankets which they set down beside Mortimer. *Turn to 478.*

104

You stop and think for a minute or two and finally figure out how you might relock the door. You try one experiment, then another, before you hear a click: the door is secure again. You sigh in relief. It would have been embarrassing — and perhaps risky — to have left the door unlocked. *Turn to 136.*

105

You rise stiffly from your examination of the door, having found no sign of whether or not the bolts have been opened and the door used. *Turn to 490.*

106

Having looked over the interior of the library, you turn your attention to the various entrances. Could the thief have escaped through the gun room door? You begin to examine it.
• *If you checked Decision 20, turn to 479.*
• *Otherwise, turn to 548.*

107

You rise to your feet and look around the room, trying to find other things to search.
• *If you checked Clue AA, turn to 249.*
• *Otherwise, turn to 512.*

108

You make certain that the Captain is comfortable, then ask him: "I understand that you went straight to the drawing room, Captain?"

"Aye, lad," Leaf answers, visibly shaken. "I needed a drink very badly indeed! I have seen twenty-four of these re-creations, and I never thought I would see a man shot in one of them."

"While you were in the drawing room," you continue, "did you hear any noise from the library? Perhaps the sound of someone moving around?"

"No, I heard nothing," he answers, puzzled by your question. "Of course, we were talking quite a bit — you know Jackson. The man cannot be quiet for a second."

You ask another question or two, but learn nothing of use. Thanking Leaf for his help, you open the door for him. ***Turn to 496.***

109

"Foxx stole the eagle," you assert. "He was separated from the rest of us for a few minutes. It was quite possible that he caused the shooting to give himself the opportunity."

"No, no," Holmes says sternly. "He has no reason to commit such a crime, or to hide the eagle where he did. And it would have been folly for anybody to touch the eagle after everyone had returned from the duel — there were too many people nearby." ***Turn to 540.***

110

"Stealing the eagle was a very foolish thing to do!" the Colonel tells his niece. "It is fortunate that this gentleman found it in the dumbwaiter. If you do anything like this again, I will cut you off without a penny!"

"Yes, Uncle Alex," Ellen answers meekly, then winks at you. "But can you do something to keep Mr. Snead from leaving?"

"Oh, I shouldn't worry about that; it is too late for him to catch the train tonight," the Colonel answers. ***Turn to 579.***

111

You stop in the hall, carefully reviewing the evidence that you have gathered. The Colonel will undoubtedly ask for a solution to the various puzzles this case presents when you go downstairs.

• *If you checked Decision 21,* ***turn to 579.***
• *Otherwise,* ***turn to 300.***

112

You shake your head, admitting your ignorance. Even Jackson's information helps only a little. It is Captain Leaf who explains the motive.

"Grayson would benefit enormously from preventing the marriage of Miss Mortimer and Mr. Snead," he says. "When they marry, the happy couple will inherit a grand sum of money left in trust in the will of old Colonel Murphy, the man who commanded the battery in Spain. Grayson is the trustee. He must have relied upon our blaming the shooting on Snead; that would have shattered the engagement rather suddenly, don't you agree?" ***Turn to 165.***

113

"I accused her by the process of elimination," you say. "I do not think that any of the other suspects could possibly have taken the eagle. Therefore, Miss Dunlop must have taken the eagle."

"Well, in this case, you are correct," Holmes says. "Miss Dunlop did take the eagle, but you have presented absolutely no proof for your charge. That is very poor work indeed. You should be ashamed of yourself."

You wonder vaguely whether you can outrun the Colonel if he starts after you with the riding crop.

• *If you want to investigate the case again,* ***turn to the Prologue.***
• *If you want Holmes' explanation,* ***turn to 119.***

114

"Miss Dunlop also has keys to open the padlocks that secured the eagle," you continue. "She could have freed the eagle quickly."

"I think it is enough," Holmes says, interrupting, "although you should have found more complete proof of her guilt. You should be more careful in future investigations." *Turn to 120.*

115

"The eagle is now secure in the Colonel's safe," Holmes says, clearly pleased. "We wish to know the identity of the thief, to prevent any attempted repetition of the crime. Who stole the eagle?" the detective asks you.

As you hesitate, the Colonel repeats Holmes' question: "Yes, who did steal the eagle?"
- *If you say an outsider stole it,* **turn to 297.**
- *If you admit you do not know,* **turn to 443.**
- *If you accuse Grayson, the solicitor,* **turn to 382.**
- *If you accuse Beach, the butler,* **turn to 294.**
- *If you accuse Foxx,* **turn to 109.**
- *If you accuse Snead,* **turn to 513.**
- *If you accuse Miss Dunlop,* **turn to 199.**
- *If you accuse another servant,* **turn to 307.**
- *If you accuse Lieutenant Jackson and Captain Leaf,*
  turn to 392.

116

Watching the others out of the corner of your eye, you realize from their actions that many of the guests appear very tense. Mortimer, Snead, Miss Mortimer and Grayson are obviously uncomfortable, and their conversation is strained and vapid. You wonder why such a highly-anticipated event as the duel has created such tension. *Pick a number and add your Intuition bonus:*
- *If 2-7,* **turn to 447.**
- *If 8-12,* **turn to 332.**

117

You continue to examine the pistols. They are clean and empty, ready for use. As you carefully examine them, you see a tiny mark in the butt of each gun. You gently scratch it with a fingernail, and a small compartment opens. You find nothing in the secret compartment of either gun and return them to their case. *Turn to 426.*

118

Recalling the grey mud you found on the ladder in the library, you wonder whether you should check Foxx's shoes.
• *If you examine the shoes, turn to 527.*
• *Otherwise, turn to 575.*

119

"But then how can you say my niece stole the eagle?" the Colonel roars. "You have not presented a single piece of evidence to support your insulting claim."

"The evidence is obvious," Holmes says didactically. "Good detective work should have uncovered it. When I examined the library ladder, I found greyish-colored mud. Outside, I found a patch of mud of that color, beside the path leading to the duelling ground. Only one person ran through the mud. From what I learned by my questioning, I am convinced that your niece was the only person who ran through the mud instead of staying on the path. In addition, when I searched her room, I found mud on her shoes that matched that on the ladder."

Holmes pauses to allow the Colonel a moment to process the proof he has offered. "That evidence should be sufficient. In addition, the thief must have known the house very well. Other evidence suggests that the thief was not very strong, another fact that would point to your niece." *Turn to 120.*

The outraged red fades from the Colonel's face as he hears the evidence. With his face paling, he sags into his chair. "But why?" he asks in a broken voice. "Why would she steal it? She has no reason to do such a thing. I have done everything for her that I could."

"What do you think?" Holmes asks you.

- *If she stole it for her fiance,* ***turn to 511.***
- *If she stole it for the money,* ***turn to 122.***
- *If she stole it to prevent anyone from leaving the house,* ***turn to 123.***
- *If she stole it to hurt her uncle,* ***turn to 132.***

121

"The thief had an accomplice," you boldly announce. "After he stole the eagle, he carried it to the drawing room and passed it to the other man, who waited outside. I am afraid that the standard is long gone."

"Nonsense!" Holmes snaps, startling you. "You have not examined the matter with sufficient care. Redruth was working outside the drawing room all morning. He would have seen any such transaction and stopped it, for he is a loyal servant."

"Then where is the eagle?" the Colonel asks, exasperated by the delay.

"Come to the library and I shall show you," Holmes answers, leading the way. *Turn to 310.*

122

"I think Miss Dunlop desired the money she could get for the eagle," you say. "She stole the bird for her own personal gain."

"Nonsense!" Holmes says. "Why should she do that? There is no evidence suggesting that she needs money. I am certain that her uncle is very generous in that regard. And aside from that, how would a young lady of gentle upbringing know how to dispose of stolen goods? Your assertion is insulting as well as stupid." *Turn to 138.*

"I think 'stole' may be the wrong word for your niece's actions," you say to the baffled Colonel. "I think she hid the eagle, probably because she knew that you would let no one leave while it was missing."

"But why would she do such a thing?" the Colonel demands, obviously disturbed and confused by his niece's actions.

"Your niece is a young romantic," Holmes answers, "and she was distressed to see her friend Susan Mortimer's engagement broken. She hoped that if Snead and the Mortimers were forced to remain here, a reconciliation would occur. It is an illogical reason for grand theft, but then, women have been known to be quite illogical at times." ***Turn to 142.***

124

You have failed completely to solve the mystery of the shooting. Pounding your desk in frustration, you wonder how to proceed now.

• *If you wish to begin the case again,* ***turn to the Prologue.***

• *Otherwise, you retire to Cornwall to raise sheep. The End*

125

Trying to appear casual, you wander near the Mortimers. They make no attempt to hide the subject of their conversation. Obviously the parents are unhappy that their daughter is going to marry a man she has known only a month or two, especially as the couple will live on the other side of the Atlantic.

"I understand your concern, I really do," the daughter acknowledges, "but I have no doubts of my fiance's good character. Robert and I should be thrilled by your blessing, which we pray for daily." *Check Deduction 13.* ***Turn to 320.***

126

As the time for the duel draws near, you find you can pay little attention to your book. Near eleven-thirty, the other guests leave in a group: the officers strut in their uniforms, while Snead and Mortimer wear the flashy scarlet uniforms from the days of Waterloo. The group shows a strange mix of solemnity and eager anticipation of the event. You remember that the exchange of shots is scheduled for five minutes after noon. A little later, Grayson comes through the drawing room on his way out.

"Good day, sir," he says pleasantly. "I am going into town to send a telegram and wonder if I might do anything for you or Dr. Watson. I've decided to take the shorter way through the woods, as the weather is so pleasant," the solicitor says, pointing vaguely through the French windows toward the nearby trees. Thanking him, you hand Grayson a note for Holmes and watch him go.

• *If you follow him,* ***turn to 586.***
• *Otherwise,* ***turn to 160.***

You join Captain Leaf in the corner; he is refilling his glass with port. The veteran is obviously pleased to have a new audience, and he begins to assault you with a series of tales, alternating stories of court life with reminiscences of odd things he saw in his twenty years of army service. Carefully, you try to turn the conversation to your fellow guests, to see if you can learn anything of use. ***Pick a number*** *and add your* *Communication bonus:*
• *If 2-5,* ***turn to 283.***
• *If 6-12,* ***turn to 388.***

128

Gradually the tea breaks up, and the other guests drift out of the library. As Beach, the butler, supervises the other servants tidying the room, the Colonel beckons to you. "You have never visited Eagle Towers, before," he says genially. "Would you like me to show you around?" Naturally you accept the offer, and the Colonel leads you through the side portal into the drawing room. After you compliment him on his collection of portraits and wood carvings, he leads you out another door and into a gun room.

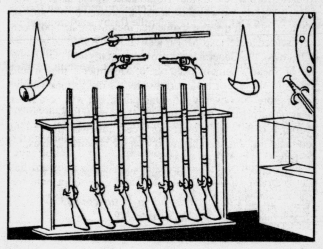

The gun room is a long, narrow room, running along the back of the house. Many old weapons, ranging from medieval longbows to Brown Bess muskets, line the inside walls, lit by three windows in the back wall. Racks of rifles and shotguns fill the wall between the windows. A glass-fronted cupboard stands at the far end. It contains several pistols surrounding a pair of duelling pistols in a walnut case lined with green velvet. As the Colonel talks of the history of many of the weapons, you glance around the room. *Pick a number* and *add your Observation bonus:*
• *If 2-7, turn to 487.*
• *If 8-12, turn to 359.*

129

"What did you mean when you said that they will have a surprise once they marry?" you ask Captain Leaf.

"You must promise not to repeat what I tell you," he says, squinting his eyes mysteriously; you nod eagerly. Leaf leads the way to an even smaller room, making sure that no one is around, and closes the door. "This is a matter of the utmost secrecy," he begins. "At the time of the original duel, Colonel Robert Murphy, the former commander of the battery, was nearing his end. He was enormously impressed by the story of the duel, but felt it was a shame that the quarrel had not been fully settled by a Snead-Mortimer wedding. As he had no heirs of his own, the General left a provision in his will that if ever one of Snead's heirs married one of Mortimer's, they would immediately inherit his entire estate. As the fortune is now worth more than twenty thousand pounds, it will be a most pleasant surprise for the young folk. But it must be kept secret, of course, or they might marry for greed, not love. And I might add that Grayson, the chap who won the shooting contest, is the trustee of the Brooks estate."

Catching your breath, you thank Leaf and promise to keep the secret. *Check Clue L.*
• *If you go back to watch the billiards, turn to 233.*
• *If you take a walk outside, turn to 449.*

130

"Perhaps Phillips' behaviour has been a little suspicious," you concede, tamping the tobacco in your pipe. Watson seems amused by your parody of Holmes' contemplative behavior. "When you are protecting something as valuable as the eagle, it is unpleasant to note any suspicious figures lurking in the background. But it would be all but impossible for an outsider to rob this house. The servants have been employed by the Colonel for years, and Beach is conscientious regarding locking all doors and windows at night."

• *If you checked Clue M,* ***turn to 418.***
• *Otherwise,* ***turn to 433.***

131

You and Leaf watch the men complete the billiards match, a closely-fought contest. Watson wins with his last shot and smiles as he pockets a shilling of Dr. Cunningham's money. Then you and the cheerful victor go up to your room together, chatting about the wonderful evening. ***Turn to 145.***

132

"Obviously Miss Dunlop did not steal the eagle to sell," you mutter, "she would not know how. I think she must have wished to upset her uncle for some reason. Perhaps some problem related to her own engagement?" you add, glancing at the colonel.

"Nonsense!" the Colonel says angrily.

Holmes interrupts him. "Quite right Colonel," he says. ***Turn to 138.***

133

As you try to sneak up on the intruder, you slip on a small rug. Staggering for a moment, you wave your hand for balance and knock over a small table. The cloaked intruder jumps at the noise, then extinguishes the lantern and dives through an open window beside him. You hurry to the window and look out but see no one. *Turn to 361.*

134

As soon as you step into Miss Dunlop's room, you see that you are in someone's permanent home, rather than a guest room. The furniture is solid and fine, with lacy cloths covering the tops of the dresser and the bedside table. A number of small paintings of birds and flowers are arranged on one wall, and the soft, pink curtains at the windows were obviously purchased for this particular person. There is a bookcase filled with novels against one wall, and a small desk in a corner. You look around, searching for possible clues. *Pick a number and add your Observation bonus:*

- *If 2-6, turn to 231.*
- *If 7-12, turn to 352.*

135

In spite of the huge dinner you have eaten (and its accompanying wine), you gather your wits and turn your attention to the conversation. Soon you realize that the cheerful talk of most of the guests is marred by some tension between Harris and Colonel Dunlop. You wonder if the problem is serious enough to threaten the wedding ceremony, since you already know that the Colonel does not fully trust his niece's fiance. *Check Deduction 9.* **Turn to 302.**

136

After completing your examination of the door, you and Watson sneak downstairs. An arched doorway leads from the hall into the library, but you can see that a gate bars the way, held shut by a chain and heavy padlock.

You carefully test the gate and find that it is sound. 'Shall I try to pick the lock?' you wonder. At the drawing room entrance, you see that the gate is identical to the one leading from the hall. If one gate can be opened, then either could be. There is less chance of being seen if you test the drawing room entrance.

• *If you try to open the lock,* **turn to 184.**
• *Otherwise,* **turn to 393.**

137

Entranced by the promise of the pamphlet, you avidly begin to read the jewel thief's account of his criminal experiences. The pamphlet is filled with information about many daring thefts, but you recognize that he reveals little that you do not know. In the tract, the author explains that most thefts arise from the foolishness of the victims and comments that a burglar should always look for items which will be valuable when rendered into their component parts. For example, it is almost always too dangerous to attempt to sell a famous piece of art or jewelry.

Bored after fifteen minutes, you toss the pamphlet aside and drift off to sleep. As the train's brakes squeal and the engine slows, you awaken to see Doctor Watson putting away his book. **Turn to 329.**

"Then why did she take it, Holmes?" a frustrated Watson asks.

"She stole it because she is a romantic," Holmes answers. "She saw her friend's engagement broken by this unfortunate incident today, and realized that if Mr. Snead left, there would be no chance for a reconciliation.Therefore, she created a situation that would keep Snead and the Mortimers here. Obviously, Colonel Dunlop would permit no one to leave while the eagle was missing." *Turn to 142.*

139

Phillips is quite small; you anticipate an easy fight. Grappling and rolling on the ground, you intend to overwhelm him with your weight. Instead, he escapes and springs back to his feet. As you try to follow, he trips you with a quick kick. You stumble forward, and he buries a knee in your belly. Gasping in agony, you fall to the ground. The poacher is long gone before you can get to your feet.

Brushing leaves and twigs from your clothes, you smile a little at your failure. At least he did you no lasting harm, and no one saw him best you. *Turn to 413.*

140

You find Colonel Dunlop seated in the library, pretending to read. You explain your discovery to him, and he nods in satisfaction.

"That must be the cause," he says, controlling his voice with an effort. "I happen to know that Grayson is strapped for cash. Perhaps he must maintain control of the trust money to avoid financial ruin. Leave the resolution of the matter to me."

In a matter of a quarter of an hour, you are told that Mr. Grayson has departed on urgent family business. The weekend flies by, and on Monday morning you return to London with Holmes and Watson. At 221 Baker Street, the great detective congratulates you on your success and your increasing skill. As Holmes and Watson chat about other affairs, you sit back to savor your success, already wondering — what challenge will my next case bring? The End

141

You remember that the dumbwaiter no longer functions, and that this is the only entrance to it. Even if the thief tried to use it, he could not have sent the eagle anywhere by the dumbwaiter.

• *If you look inside the dumbwaiter, turn to 476.*
• *Otherwise, turn to 224.*

142

The conversation lags for a minute, then Watson says: "The theft of the eagle was a small thing; what I do not understand is the shooting of Lieutenant Mortimer. Who was responsible for the shooting — and why?"

"Yes," the Colonel adds, "who loaded the duelling pistol with a real bullet?"

"Oh, I imagine our friend can explain the matter," Holmes says, looking at you. You think for a moment before offering your solution.

• *If you do not know, turn to 147.*
• *If you name Snead, turn to 148.*
• *If you name Foxx, turn to 168.*
• *If you name Grayson, turn to 173.*
• *If you name Captain Leaf, turn to 175.*
• *If you name Mortimer, turn to 183.*
• *If you name the Colonel, turn to 186.*
• *If you say no one did, turn to 202.*

143

Overcoming your momentary shock, you charge from your hiding place and tackle Grayson, who exhales sharply as you knock him down. The rifle fires as he falls under your charge, the shot going wide. With everybody charging up to you, Grayson makes no attempt to fight.

"What's going on?" the Colonel demands in an angry voice. "What is the meaning of this interruption?" You and Grayson try to explain. *Pick a number and add your Communication bonus:*

• *If 2-6, turn to 458.*
• *If 7-12, turn to 517.*

Ignoring your threat, Phillips dives at you, knocking you down in the brush. Locked in each other's arms, you and the poacher grapple desperately for an advantage, rolling over and over in the prickly brush. *Pick a number and add your Athletics bonus:*

• *If 2-7, turn to 139.*
• *If 8-12, turn to 295.*

145

Alone in the room with Watson, you sit to chat, relaxing in a dressing gown and slippers.

"I am not at all certain that we have a case," Watson comments, between puffs on his pipe. "None of our fellow guests has acted suspiciously, to my eyes."

"Is that so?" you reply, deliberately ambiguous.

"Consider them one by one, and tell me which one could possibly be a thief," Watson challenges. "This fellow Harris, for example, hardly seems to be a dishonest man, for all the Colonel's suspicions."

• *If you checked Deduction 6, turn to 441.*
• *Otherwise, turn to 163.*

146

Having completed a search of the room, you go out in the hall. Before going downstairs, you stop to think for a moment. *Turn to 111.*

147

The silence is overwhelming for a few seconds. Finally you summon the courage to say: "I do not know who loaded the duelling pistols, or why they were loaded. I was not able to uncover enough evidence to be certain who did it."

"Very good," Holmes says, surprising you with his mildness. "It is far better to admit your failure than to randomly accuse an innocent person." *Turn to 188.*

148

"Mr. Snead is the only person who could have loaded the pistol," you say. "I think he is the only one who should be considered in the matter."

"Why are you certain?" Holmes asks.
• *If you checked both Clue R and Clue DD, turn to 149.*
• *If you checked Clue R but not Clue DD, turn to 554.*
• *If you checked Clue DD but not Clue R, turn to 581.*
• *If you checked neither Clue R nor Clue DD, turn to 583.*

149

"I have evidence to support the accusation," you say confidently. "I found balls that would fit the duelling pistols hidden in Mr. Snead's trunk. Also, I watched carefully when the guns were loaded. No one else had the chance to do anything to them before they were handed to the duellists. Therefore, Snead is the only man who could have put the slug in his pistol."

"A very sound explanation," Holmes says, and you smile for a moment at the compliment. "Unfortunately, you are wrong, very wrong indeed." *Turn to 188.*

150

Though you go over it inch by inch, you find no useful evidence on the ladder. You must search elsewhere to find clues to the identity of the thief. *Turn to 428.*

151

With every nerve on edge, you move stealthily towards the location of the noise. You hope that the intruder has hidden in a way that will keep him from seeing you. You reach the couch, peer over it and see the intruder running for a hole in the wall. You laugh softly to yourself — it was only a small mouse. *Turn to 272.*

152

Now that you have the gun room to yourself, you turn your attention to the door leading into the library. You try to pick the lock and quietly shake it. You cannot open or unlock it; the bolts on the other side would prevent you even if you could pick the lock. Satisfied that you have looked into every aspect of the room's security, you rejoin Watson and return to your room. You practically fall into bed, hearing Watson's comforting snores just before you fall asleep. *Turn to 187.*

153

You look around the room once more and try to decide if there is anything else worth examining.
• *If you checked Clue AA, turn to 209.*
• *Otherwise, turn to 146.*

154

You talk to Harris for a few minutes, trying to steer the conversation to topics such as what Harris does with his time, but the task is made quite difficult by Miss Dunlop's affectionate presence. *Pick a number and add your Communication bonus:*
• *If 2-8, turn to 580.*
• *If 9-12, turn to 455.*

155

You dismiss the movement from your mind. It must have been a bird or a small animal scurrying through the brush. You wonder what it is about this duel that makes you so uneasy. *Turn to 320.*

156

"The gunman must have intended to break up the marriage," you confidently conclude. "He would have been able to find a much better opportunity to hurt Mortimer or Snead if that had been his desire. And as we saw, the wounding almost prevented the marriage, for Susan Mortimer's parents wanted to find some reason to break the engagement, even before the duel."

"But Mortimer's parents did not shoot at him," Holmes replies. "Why would someone would want to stop the marriage?"

"Foxx was formerly engaged to Susan Mortimer," Watson says, "but he was with us. He could not have fired the shot."

You consider the question.

• *If you checked Clue L, turn to 516.*
• *Otherwise, turn to 452.*

157

Hardly daring to breath for fear of losing your balance, you shuffle along the molding until you reach the mantle. There you study the security surrounding the eagle. The golden bird is mounted on a heavy block of polished walnut, which has steel rings attached to each corner. Chains run through these rings and are fastened to rings in the mantle itself by heavy padlocks. Aside from the difficulty of reaching the mantle, a thief would have to be able to pick these formidable locks. *Pick a number* and add your Scholarship bonus:

• *If 2-7, turn to 355.*
• *If 8-12, turn to 358.*

158

You follow the path toward the clearing where the duel was staged. Your memory of the path is clear and correct. It runs straight until it reaches the muddy patch, then curves to avoid the boggy ground. Virtually everyone must have avoided the mud — only one set of footprints appears to have crossed it, and these are too blurred to identify. However, they definitely lead from the duelling grounds back to the house. That one person must be the thief! You try to decide who it was.

- *If you think it was the Colonel, **turn to 470.***
- *If you think it was Snead, **turn to 472.***
- *If you think it was Captain Leaf, **turn to 475.***
- *If you think it was Lieutenant Jackson, **turn to 477.***
- *If you think it was Harris, **turn to 482.***
- *If you think it was Ellen Dunlop, **turn to 267.***
- *If you think it was Dr. Watson, **turn to 491.***
- *If you think it was Dr. Cunningham, **turn to 493.***
- *If you do not know, **turn to 495.***

159

You join everyone else in running to Mortimer's side. Amidst the screams and excited talk, the group has just enough sense to let the two doctors attend to the wounded man. Mortimer is bleeding from the back of his neck and appears to be dazed.

"How bad is it, doctor?" Miss Mortimer asks in a desperate voice verging on hysteria.

"Not as bad as it looks," Dr. Cunningham says as he bandages the wound. "The shot just scraped the back of his neck and went on. The wound may stun him for a moment and can bleed badly, but the young man will be fine in a day or two."

As the others express their relief, you hear Mrs. Mortimer tell her daughter: "I'll be damned if I shall allow you to marry some half-cocked foreigner who tried to shoot your brother!"

You study the scene, trying to understand how this could have happened.

- *If you talk to Dr. Watson about the wound, **turn to 486.***
- *Otherwise, **turn to 185.***

160

You sit in the house reading, keeping one ear cocked for movement in the library. A little after noon, Harris wanders by and goes outside through the open French windows. You are alone in the house with the servants and the eagle.

• *If you check on the eagle, **turn to 259.***
• *Otherwise, **turn to 339.***

161

"I see nothing to indicate which of you is travelling," you admit, embarrassed.

"You mean that you cannot interpret what you see," Holmes says. "I must assume that you are not blind. These bags bear the customs marks of France and Sweden. You should recall that I have visited both those countries recently, while Watson has remained in England since his marriage."

"It is always so simple, once you explain," you remark, blushing. "But if I am such a dolt, why did you send for me?" ***Turn to 317.***

162

Try as you might, you cannot secure the lock again. After several failed attempts, you admit failure. At least no one else can open this door! *Check Decision 7.* ***Turn to 136.***

163

"Having met the man," Watson continues, "I cannot support the Colonel's suspicions of Harris at all. He seems a very pleasant young fellow, spending the weekend here with his charming fiance. A young man in love would hardly rob his fiance's family, even if he were a thief."

You note Watson's comments, then say: "You usually see the best in a chap, John. Consider the thieves you have known — were all of them unpleasant men who would never think of doing something so uncourteous as robbing their in-laws?"

"But Harris seems... all right," Watson insists. "I have seen him do nothing suspicious."

• *If you checked Deduction 5, **turn to 311.***
• *Otherwise, **turn to 400.***

Casually you glance around the library again, impressed by the number and variety of books on the shelves. Then, something catches your eye near the fireplace. Partially screened by a chair, there is a small hatch two feet square. Only a child could enter it easily, but you wonder where it might lead, and why it was built there.

"What's that small hatch?" you ask the Colonel. "Could someone use it?"

"No, no, it's not good for anything," he answers. "That used to be a dumbwaiter, but it doesn't work any longer. My father rearranged the kitchen and blocked the hatch in the basement, and we also blocked up the opening upstairs. In addition to the fact that it leads nowhere, it doesn't work properly. When you work the ropes, it won't go down at all, and it stops halfway to the upper floor if you pull it up. If a thief somehow climbed into that thing, he would be capturing himself for us." He laughs heartily. *Check Clue C.* **Turn to 344.**

Later that afternoon, you and Watson drive into Gunston to dine with Holmes, who looks wan and tired. Smoking heavily, the detective listens carefully to you, deeply interested in your methods.

"You have not solved the case completely on your own," Holmes says sternly, "but you managed to prevent a serious crime and enabled others to bring the truth out. Your actions brought the investigation to a successful conclusion."

He then tells you and Watson how he solved the jewel thefts in Devon and Cornwall, but as you listen, your thoughts drift away.

'When will my next case unfold?' you wonder. The End

"I think that the eagle is hidden in the dumbwaiter, in the library," you say.

"How could that be?" the Colonel asks, his eyes wide with disbelief. "It does not lead anywhere."

"It would thus be the perfect hiding place," Watson says.

"Let us look and see," Holmes interrupts, and you all hurry to the library.

• *If you checked Deduction 25,* ***turn to 356.***
• *Otherwise,* ***turn to 331.***

You study the undamaged locks and then drop them back onto the mantle. They do not provide you with any clue to the theft of the eagle. ***Turn to 177.***

"I think Foxx loaded the pistol," you say. "He slipped a bullet into it when he loaded them with powder. Perhaps he hoped to disgrace Snead and win back Miss Mortimer's affections. "

"That is impossible!" Watson says suddenly. "I watched every move Foxx made as he loaded the pistols. He had no chance to slip a ball into one."

"Very good, Watson," Holmes says. "You saved me the trouble of defending the fellow's innocence." ***Turn to 188.***

"I think Holmes would examine the library," you say, sighing a little, for you are tired. Watson looks unhappy, but nods agreement. You sleep for two or three hours, arising again between one and two o'clock in the morning.

The house is quiet. You lead Watson into the hall and move slowly towards the stairs. You first stop by the door in the hall that leads into the library gallery. It is locked.

• *If you try to pick the lock,* ***turn to 407.***
• *Otherwise,* ***turn to 136.***

170

Concentrating carefully, you slip the piece of metal into the lock and wriggle it. After a moment the padlock pops open. Smiling a little, you close it and return the object to the table. *Check Clue CC.* **Turn to 442.**

171

A thick-cushioned chair near the fireplace holds a hollowed spot in the middle of the cushion. You compare its position to the ladder and the mantle and deduce that the thief dropped the eagle into the chair before climbing back down the ladder. Why would the thief do such a thing? **Pick a number** *and add your Intuition bonus:*
• *If 2-7,* **turn to 238.**
• *If 8-12,* **turn to 326.**

172

You begin to examine the ladder very carefully. Perhaps the thief left some evidence behind. **Pick a number** *and add your Observation bonus: (Add 2 if you have the magnifying glass.)*
• *If 2-7,* **turn to 150.**
• *If 8-12,* **turn to 489.**

173

"I think Grayson, the solicitor, loaded the pistols earlier," you say. "He avoided the duel to provide an alibi."

"Oh, nonsense!" the Colonel snaps. "Dr. Watson and I examined both guns just before we took them down to the duelling grounds. Neither was loaded at that time." **Turn to 188.**

You decide to spend the evening in the library, to be certain of the safety of the eagle. There is a comfortable chair in a corner, hidden from the hall entrance by shelves that jut from the wall. You examine the shelves until you find a book Watson recommended to you — *Dawns and Departures of a Soldier's Life* — and settle down to read it. You bury yourself in the book, and the evening seems to fly by. It is past ten when you here voices from the hallway, and two men enter the room. You sit quietly, wondering if you might learn something of interest.

"That eagle is a torment to me, Jackson," you hear Grayson say. "If I owned such a trinket, I could raise all the cash that I would need. Think of the comfort and security that would give me!"

"It is unfortunate that your father didn't have the sense to collect a few souvenirs when he was in India," Jackson says, and you hear their footsteps leaving the room again.

A few minutes later Watson comes in to see if you are prepared to retire for the evening. He glances at your book, laughs and says: "I told you you'd enjoy it, didn't I?" Reluctantly you return the book to its place and go up to your room with Watson. *Check Clue K.* **Turn to 145.**

175

"I think Captain Leaf loaded the guns," you say. "He must have found an opportunity to do it amid all the talk before the duel."

"You have no evidence," Holmes answers, "nor a single motive for Leaf to do such a thing. Do not waste our time with baseless charges!" **Turn to 188.**

176

You carefully examine Snead's shoes. The pair he wore to the duel are still damp, and odd bits of grass are stuck to them. There is no sign of the mud, however. They therefore provide no evidence that Snead was the thief. **Turn to 566.**

177

You climb down the ladder and look around the library. It might have been difficult for a thief to take the eagle from the library, considering the number of people nearby. You carefully look under and behind all the furniture in the library. You do not find the eagle. You stop to think for a moment, wondering if the thief might have left other evidence of his passage. You methodically walk around the room, looking at every couch and chair, trying to find some mark left by the thief. *Pick a number* and *add your Observation bonus:*
• *If 2-7, turn to 435.*
• *If 8-12, turn to 171.*

178

"I have no solid grounds for suspicion," you admit, "but I do not believe that you can eliminate a suspect simply because of his age or profession. Note, however, cousin John, that I do not claim Grayson to be a prime suspect." *Turn to 378.*

179

Excusing yourself to refill your teacup and to take another biscuit, you reflect upon the conflicts already apparent. It is clear to you that Foxx still loves Miss Mortimer and that he regrets the ending of their engagement. He is obviously jealous of Snead. You wonder if Foxx might try to hurt or humiliate the Canadian over the course of the weekend. *Check Deduction 2. Turn to 471.*

180

You consider the other witnesses. It is of little value to question Snead and Foxx, for if they went straight upstairs, as they claim, they saw nothing. If one of them is the thief, he is not likely to tell you the truth anyway. On another note, Miss Dunlop was very busy when she returned to the house, but she is a sharp, intelligent lady. Perhaps she noticed something.
• *If you question Miss Dunlop, turn to 191.*
• *Otherwise, turn to 483.*

181

For a moment you wonder how the ladder came to be in the library. Then you remember that you saw it before. The Colonel keeps it in a corner so that, if necessary, he may get books from the upper shelves. You wonder what clues it might reveal. *Turn to 172.*

182

You decide that it is necessary to search upstairs. The Colonel reluctantly agrees with the idea. You put one of the padlocks from the eagle's chain in your pocket. If you find some sort of key or lockpick, you can try it without calling attention to yourself.
• *If you checked Decision 21, turn to 420.*
• *Otherwise, turn to 533.*

183

"Miss Mortimer loaded the gun," you say. "She must have secretly wanted out of the her engagement, and knew that the gun going off would make that hidden desire a reality."

"Nonsense!" say the Colonel and Watson. Holmes adds, "There is no evidence that that young woman is cold-blooded enough to risk her brother's life in such a way. Think before you speak, sir; think before you speak!" *Turn to 188.*

184

You bend over the padlock and examine it. With the proper tools, you could probably open it easily, even though it is very heavy and impressive in appearance. Quickly you start to work. *Pick a number* and add your Artifice bonus: (Add 4 if you have the skeleton keys.)
• *If 2-9, turn to 459.*
• *If 10-12, turn to 365.*

185

Amidst the excited talk of all the others, you try to review the situation. Has some important clue been overlooked? *Pick a number* and add your Intuition bonus:
• *If 2-9, turn to 103.*
• *If 10-12, turn to 322.*

186

"You loaded the pistol, Colonel," you say. "Though as to why you did it, I cannot hazard a guess."

The Colonel grabs his riding crop and starts towards you. "Patience, Colonel," Holmes says, holding up a hand to halt the enraged old man, "we almost forced our friend to accuse someone. It is just as well that he made an absurd accusation, rather than blaming someone who might be connected to the crime by a shred of evidence." *Turn to 188.*

187

The footman bringing you hot water and morning tea wakes you the next morning. You rise eagerly, dressing and shaving quickly while you sip the tea. Bright sunlight streams in through the windows, and a fresh breeze makes the beautiful day even more stimulating. Watson is soon ready, and you go down to breakfast together.

• If you checked Decision 7, *turn to 543.*
• Otherwise, *turn to 309.*

188

"Holmes, enough of this suspense!" Watson snaps. "I know you must build the scene to display your cleverness, but please tell us who was responsible."

"Oh, very well, Watson," Holmes answers with a chuckle. "But our friend should not be embarrassed." You nod, indicating your thanks. "There is a very good reason why he could not identify the individual who loaded the duelling pistol with live ammunition."

• If you wish to investigate the case again, *turn to the Prologue.*
• If you want to hear Holmes' explanation, *turn to 194.*

189

You work at the door for some time, trying to find a way to spring the lock. Watson watches you anxiously, but his concern is of no help. After ten minutes of effort you shrug your shoulders and turn away.

"No one can pick this lock," you whisper to Watson. "I should wager my career upon it." Your cousin gives you a questioning look. *Turn to 136.*

190

You follow the path for some distance, but you find no evidence of the gunman. He has escaped you for the moment. Disappointed, you return to the house with the others. ***Turn to 525.***

191

You see that Miss Dunlop is comfortably seated and relaxed before you begin to question her. "What I need to study," you explain, "are the movements of each person while separated from the others. Now, you ran up to the house by yourself, to get more help for Mortimer. Did you see anyone in or near the house then?"
• *If you checked Decision 26,* ***turn to 499.***
• *Otherwise,* ***turn to 519.***

You stand near the table and watch Foxx load the pistols, looking for any unusual action or movement. Then Foxx takes a powder horn and tips some of the contents down the barrel of each pistol, tapping it with the ramrod. He then takes a piece of paper and rams that down on top of the powder to hold it in place. Then Foxx picks up a smaller horn, using it to fill the priming pan of each gun. The task completed, he carefully caps the horns and returns the weapons to their places in the case. ***Pick a number*** *and add your Observation bonus:*
• *If 2-7,* ***turn to 423.***
• *If 8-12,* ***turn to 587.***

193

"Now for a truly suspicious character," Watson continues, "you would have to search far and wide to find a better suspect than that poacher, what's-his-name? Phillips!"

"Come now, John," you reply, "it is a long stretch from poaching to jewel theft."

"Perhaps," replies Watsom, "but it is far from impossible. I am not certain, but I believe I saw him lurking in the bushes tonight, watching the house. What do you think of that, cousin?"
• *If you checked Deduction 11,* ***turn to 524.***
• *Otherwise,* ***turn to 130.***

194

"Nobody put a bullet in the duelling pistol," Holmes announces flatly. The others stare at him for a second.

"Nonsense!" the Colonel snaps. "I saw one man fire and the other fall bleeding from the shot. What do you mean?"

"Yes, Holmes," Watson adds, "You really must explain what you mean."

"You did not see what occurred, however," Holmes answers. "I knew Snead was not responsible as soon as you described the wound to me. Think of how a man stands ready for a duel. He points his side toward his opponent and turns his head to face him. It would be physically impossible for a shot from Snead's gun to have scraped the back of Mortimer's neck." ***Turn to 536.***

195

"What are you doing here?" you ask Phillips again.

Before replying, the little man gathers his wind. "I was looking for that Mortimer bloke," he growls, "the one what dragged me to the Colonel last night. He ought to know better than that, sir. He's a country gentleman, just like the Colonel. He's no cause to be doing gamekeeper's work. Now if Colonel Dunlop laid hands on me while I'm laying my snares, or if his men caught me, I'd take my punishment like a man. But it's not right when a houseguest starts acting like a gamekeeper when he has no cause to, am I right? "

The man continues his complaints for sometime. Satisfied that you have learned everything he has to say, you tell him he can go. Defeated, Phillips grabs his cap and vanishes into the woods. How honest is he? *Check Deduction 11.* **Turn to 413.**

196

You realize that only a few people could have taken the eagle. The four people who left the group early are Snead, Jackson, Leaf and Foxx. Then there is Harris, who was not at the duel, and Miss Dunlop, who came back to the house alone. The Colonel orders these six to answer your questions, and you ask each of them what he did upon returning to the house. The answers vary. Captain Leaf and Lieutenant Jackson headed straight for the drawing room and the brandy, needing a stiffener after the shooting. Snead and Foxx both say they went straight upstairs to change their shoes, though they did not go together. Harris apparently has not returned from his walk. Miss Dunlop explains that she went up to change only after Mortimer was carried to the house and settled in his bed. You decide to question some of them alone; the Colonel grants you the use of his study.

• *If you wish to question Leaf further,* **turn to 108.**

• *Otherwise,* **turn to 496.**

197

The carved hardwood molding is very beautiful, but to your distress, you see that it is only four inches wide. You have chosen a very tricky task, but you are not willing to quit now that you have begun. At least the couches beside the fireplace might break your fall if you fail. ***Pick a number*** *and add your Athletics bonus:*

• *If 2-4,* ***turn to 514.***
• *If 5-6,* ***turn to 389.***
• *If 7-9,* ***turn to 528.***
• *If 10-12,* ***turn to 157.***

198

"So you see, Mr. Holmes," you conclude, "we have solid, factual proof that Grayson shot Mortimer. But we are anxious to discover why Grayson shot him. Is he a madman or a clever, evil man?"

• *If you checked Clue L,* ***turn to 464.***
• *Otherwise,* ***turn to 218.***

199

You glance at the Colonel, knowing that he will not like what you must say. "I am afraid that your niece, Ellen, stole the eagle," you venture, eyes averted. The Colonel's face turns bright red, and he reaches for a riding crop that sits on his desk.

"How dare you say such a thing?" he thunders, threatening you.

"Patience, Colonel," Holmes says gently. "My friend must have grounds for the charge. Please reveal them to us."

• *If you checked Deduction 22,* ***turn to 346.***
• *Otherwise,* ***turn to 324.***

200

Deciding that you have followed Grayson long enough, you turn around and return to Eagle Towers. Once more you pick up your book and try to lose yourself in its bloodstained pages. ***Turn to 160.***

201

"That sounds like solid proof," Holmes admits, grudgingly, "but did you find any other evidence as well?"

You think through what you have learned.

• *If you checked Clue EE,* **turn to 398.**
• *Otherwise,* **turn to 506.**

202

"No one put a bullet in Snead's gun," you say confidently.

"What! What do you mean?" the Colonel gasps. "Are you insane, man? I saw the shot fired myself."

"Perhaps you should explain," Holmes says.

• *If you checked Clue T,* **turn to 207.**
• *Otherwise,* **turn to 260.**

203

Your examination pays off. A piece of heavy black thread is wrapped around the bottom bolt. This is the kind of clue you needed! A skilled person could have used this thread to lock the bolt from the other side of the door. Thus, someone could well have used this door to escape. *Check Clue Y.* **Turn to 490.**

204

You find Dr. Cunningham methodically practicing billiard shots, apparently trying to forget the events of the day. "I am sorry to interrupt you, doctor," you say, approaching the crouched figure diffidently, "but I am trying to uncover the underlying cause of this terrible affair. Do you know any reason why someone would want to prevent the marriage of Snead and Susan Mortimer?" The doctor sets down his cue, pausing to think. *Check Decision 16.* **Pick a number** *and add your Communication bonus: (Subtract 2 if you checked Decision 15 and/or Decision 17.)*

• *If 2-6,* **turn to 508.**
• *If 7-12,* **turn to 446.**

205

You see that as Snead raises his pistol to fire, he definitely turns the barrel away from Mortimer. *Check Clue U.* **Turn to 596.**

206

You know who will win the contest long before it is completed, even though the contestants may not know how obvious the result is. While several competitors continue for some time, only one proves to be a true dead shot. While most of the marksmen are content to just touch the target, Grayson (the solicitor) places every shot with precision. His shot strikes the center of a bit of paper stuck to the empty can; then he hits a coloured spot on the side of the apple.

When Grayson wins, you join the others in congratulating him on his accuracy. *Check Clue 1. Turn to 345.*

207

"At the same time that Snead fired his blank shot during the duel, I saw a puff of smoke rise at the edge of the woods," you say. "Someone hiding there shot Mortimer, timing the shot so that the sound blended with that of Snead's."

"Why didn't you say something at the time?" Watson demands. "Why did you let us think that Snead shot him?"

You raise a hand, asking for silence. "I was not certain of the motive for the shot, and I thought keeping quiet might give me a better chance of learning that motive."

"It still seems hard to believe," the Colonel mutters.

"Believe it, Colonel," Holmes says quietly. "I knew from the moment that Watson described the wound that there must have been a hidden marksman. A shot from one duellist could not wound another across the back of the neck." *Turn to 536.*

208

"I was watching Snead very carefully during the duel," you say. "I am certain that he aimed away from Mortimer. He could not possibly have inflicted the wound."

"Are you certain that he aimed away?" Watson asks.

"Yes," you reply. "I paid particular attention to him, and he made a point of turning his gun away before he pulled the trigger."

"Aside from that, Colonel," Holmes adds, "Snead could not have fired a shot that scraped the back of Mortimer's neck. It is physically impossible." *Turn to 536.*

209

You remember the mud from the library ladder. 'Shall I examine Miss Dunlop's shoes?' you wonder.
• *If you examine her shoes, turn to 515.*
• *Otherwise, turn to 146.*

210

Your wanderings lead you into the woods near the house, where you follow Mortimer down a path into a pleasant grove of trees. You talk a little but mostly enjoy the peaceful atmosphere of the quiet woods. *Pick a number and add your Observation bonus:*
• *If 2-7, turn to 211.*
• *If 8-12, turn to 485.*

211

Suddenly, Mortimer stops and grips your arm, motioning for you to listen. Cocking an ear in the direction he points, you hear an odd rustling among the trees. *Turn to 444.*

212

"The thief was forced to drop the eagle into a chair, rather than carry it down the ladder," you continue. "I believe this shows that the thief was not particularly strong. That evidence fits Miss Dunlop more closely than any other suspect."

"Very good," Holmes says. "You are learning your craft, sir. The evidence you have uncovered proves without a doubt that Miss Dunlop took the eagle." Watson adds his congratulations. *Turn to 120.*

213

"Come, come, man," the Colonel says in an irritated voice, "if you know something, tell us. You must have grounds for this amazing statement." You hurriedly phrase your reply.
• *If you checked Clue V, turn to 588.*
• *Otherwise, turn to 591.*

214

"So you have no evidence?" Holmes asks coldly. "It is always wise to back your conclusions with evidence. Guessing correctly is a useful talent to gypsies alone."

"How do you know that he guessed right?" Watson asks Holmes. "You were not there. We were."
• *If you want Holmes' explanation, turn to 194.*
• *If you want to investigate the case again, turn to the Prologue.*

215

Moving as quietly as possible, you try to sneak up on the intruder. You wonder what would draw someone to the gun room at two o'clock in the morning. *Pick a number and add your Artifice bonus:*
• *If 2-6, turn to 133.*
• *If 7-9, turn to 278.*
• *If 10-12, turn to 367.*

216

You wonder where the little door leads, though it doesn't seem to matter. Obviously it would be very difficult for anyone to open that door from the other side.
• *If you ask where it leads, turn to 334.*
• *Otherwise, turn to 164.*

Searching with great care, you first find a branch broken on a bush, and then uncover an ejected cartridge underneath the bush. The ground nearby is too hard for the villain's tracks to show; you begin to hunt for his escape route. *Pick a number and add your Observation bonus:*
• *If 2-7, turn to 537.*
• *If 8-12, turn to 341.*

"To determine the motive in such a case, you must look at the effect of the criminal's action," Holmes says didactically.

"The effect was rather obvious, Holmes," Watson says. "The criminal tried to kill Mortimer."

"Oh, did he?" Holmes asks, a glint of humor in his eyes. "Does it make sense to suppose that such was his purpose? You mentioned that Mortimer has walked alone outside while at Eagle Towers. If the criminal wished to kill him, he would hardly have chosen a time when there were witnesses who might see and identify him."

"Then what did he want, Mr. Holmes?" you ask, exasperated.

"It appears to me," Holmes answers, sipping at the ale, "that the marksman wanted to make you believe that Snead shot Mortimer. Now what would be the result of Mr. Snead doing such a thing, even by accident?"

"It would prevent the wedding!" you exclaim. "Mortimer's parents hardly approved of the match in any case. So I must discover who has cause to block the marriage."

"Exactly," Holmes answers. "I suggest two sources of information. You might find something in the local records in the town hall or quietly inquire of your fellow guests. I will give you a note for the custodian at the town hall — we became friends this afternoon when I pursued my own research. But be careful and tactful, or you will ensure the success of the villain's scheme. Scandal at this time might be disastrous." You thank Holmes for his advice and decide on your actions.
• *If you visit the town hall, turn to 396.*
• *If you question the other guests, turn to 273.*

Something seems a little odd in Captain Leaf's comment about the wedding. What kind of surprise can he mean? But if you ask him, you know that the captain is quite capable of burying you with a two-hour tale of his many prior adventures.
• *If you ask Captain Leaf to explain,* ***turn to 129.***
• *Otherwise,* ***turn to 131.***

220

"Robert Harris shot Mortimer," you say. "He left the house alone a little while before the duel."

"Oh, nonsense!" Holmes interjects. "You have uncovered neither evidence nor the suggestion of a motive to back this accusation."

"Aside from that," the Colonel adds angrily, "Harris is a ghastly shot. If he had aimed at Mortimer from the woods, he probably would have hit Snead. Or you!" ***Turn to 225.***

221

You wonder why there is a ladder in the library. It certainly was very convenient for the thief or thieves.
• *If you ask the Colonel about the ladder,* ***turn to 243.***
• *Otherwise,* ***turn to 172.***

Early in the morning, Beach comes to your room, wakes you, and without a word, leads you to the colonel's bedroom. On the floor by the Colonel's bed rests a pile of items used in your trap.

"Your doing?" the Colonel asks sharply. When you admit your guilt, he warns against setting any more traps. "Why, the cat might have knocked this over and awakened the entire house," he snorts. "Any burglar worth his salt would have gotten around it easily."

Chastened, you return to bed. Morning comes too soon, and you dress slowly, while an impatient Watson urges you to hurry. Finally, you are ready to go to breakfast and follow Watson down the stairs. *Turn to 599.*

223

You relax, confident that the bolts are strong. "A thief could not enter through this door," you whisper to Watson. *Check Decision 7. Turn to 136.*

224

You have finished with the ground floor section of the library and anxiously ascend the stairs to the gallery. Perhaps you can tell if the thief used the door into the upstairs hall. You go to the door and find that while the bolts and lock are secured, the key is missing from the lock. What could that mean?

• *If you checked Decision 20, turn to 412.*
• *Otherwise, turn to 411.*

225

You realize that you have failed to solve the shooting of Mortimer, although you have come close to the truth. Perhaps you should investigate the case again.

• *If you investigate the case again, turn to the Prologue.*
• *If you want to hear Holmes' explanation, turn to 228.*

Grayson walks very slowly now, moving carefully. Suddenly, he stops and spins, nearly spotting you as you dive for cover. Satisfied that he is unobserved, Grayson pauses by a hollow tree and pulls a rifle from it. With your heart pounding, the solicitor walks off; you follow him, concerned by the eagerness in Grayson's step.

Finally, he comes to the edge of a meadow and settles down in the brush, well-hidden from any watchers on the other side of the meadow. You find a good hiding place a little distance away and closely watch Grayson. You do not want to take any action until you know what he is doing. You wait for some time, your heart racing, and are then surprised to hear voices in the meadow. Peering out from your hiding place, you see most of the people from the house assembled, talking and laughing, and realize that this must be the site for the re-creation of the duel. In uniform, Snead and Mortimer take their places, only fifty yards from you. To your shock, Grayson levels his gun at Mortimer!

• *If you attack Grayson,* **turn to 143.**

• *Otherwise,* **turn to 542.**

"What did you mean," you ask Leaf, "when you mentioned the 'benefits' of Snead marrying Miss Mortimer? What benefits?" Leaf hesitates for a moment, then smiles graciously.

"You must promise not to repeat this," he says, almost whispering, and you quickly agree. "Well," he continues, "when they marry, an old will takes effect, and a trust will be paid to them, as the first Mortimer and Snead to wed. Grayson is the sole trustee, and I know he has administered the money carefully. The shooting today was probably just some damn fool hunter, firing at a rabbit without knowing that people were nearby."

You quickly thank Captain Leaf for the information and hurry to hunt Colonel Dunlop. *Check Clue L.* **Turn to 140.**

"Well, Holmes," Watson grumbles, "if my cousin is wrong, who was the hidden marksman? Knowing your superlative skills, I am certain that you have already deduced the identity of the culprit."

"Thank you for your confidence, Watson," Holmes answers, blowing smoke rings toward the high ceiling. "As it happens, I do know who fired the shot. It was Thomas Grayson, the solicitor. I have clippings on him at Baker Street. He is one of the finest shots in the country, and therefore was certain to do what he wanted — wound Mortimer slightly, in a manner that would bring blame upon Snead." *Turn to 303.*

229

"Grayson was very nervous this morning," you explain. "He had no reason to be so; thus, I think that the tension arose from his plans for the day."

"Hardly evidence," Holmes sniffs. "Hardly more than a baseless assumption. What else do you know?"

• *If you checked Clue I, turn to 241.*
• *Otherwise, turn to 281.*

230

You open the door and enter Snead's room. It reminds you of your own. Snead has a large, corner bedroom, with heavy, comfortable furniture. The bed is perfectly made. There is a large closet, whose open door shows its emptiness, a large dresser, and a big steamer trunk, closed by a heavy padlock. The key is visible in the lock. A search of the dresser reveals nothing of interest. You wonder whether you should search the chest.

• *If you search the chest, turn to 546.*
• *Otherwise, turn to 562.*

231

You go through the desk, the dresser and the wardrobe, but nothing seems to have a bearing on the case. Perhaps you have wasted your time searching this room. *Turn to 153.*

232

Leaping small bushes and ducking low limbs, you follow the alleged poacher through the woods, Mortimer a little off to your right. Though the smaller man passes among the trees like a will-o-the-wisp, you draw closer to him. Then, he stops and hesitates. Before he can start again you dive forward, ready to sweep his legs out from under him.

Unfortunately, your grasp slips, but Mortimer seizes the man before he can take advantage of your mistake. Together, you and Mortimer march the little man to the house. There, Mortimer tells the Colonel how he caught "the little fellow" poaching. ***Turn to 360.***

233

You return to the billiard room to find Watson and Dr. Cunningham battling at the table. ***Turn to 131.***

234

The challenge of discovering who might be spying on the house overcomes your doubts and fears. Would Sherlock Holmes ignore such an opportunity? You begin to move quietly through the woods, watching every step and moving with the greatest possible care. ***Pick a number*** and add your Artifice bonus:
• If 2-8, ***turn to 296.***
• If 9-12, ***turn to 523.***

235

The footman wakes you the next morning when he brings you hot water and morning tea. The bright sunlight and pleasant breeze pouring through your window act to make you forget the previous evening's embarassment. You dress and shave quickly, then hesitate. What will the other guests say?

"Oh, come along now," Watson says, putting a hand around your shoulder. "You must face them sometime, and the sooner you do so, the sooner it will be forgotten." Sighing apprehensively, you agree and go down to breakfast. Your fellow guests are surprisingly cheerful.

"Ahh, here's the high-wire performer," Mortimer jests, as Snead and Foxx bow to greet you. Their ease with each other is surprising in rivals for the hand of the same lady. "My young friend, are you satisfied the eagle is safe?" the Colonel inquires, loading his plate with bacon and eggs. You go to the side table and begin to fill your own plate, relieved at the others' reaction. It is obvious that none of your fellow guests is irritated by your presence — yet. ***Turn to 309.***

236

While the others wait, you continue to review the evidence in your mind. You know that it is very important to explain your proof clearly.
• *If you checked Deduction 19,* ***turn to 551.***
• *Otherwise,* ***turn to 340.***

237

"Yes," the Colonel urges, "tell us why you accuse Grayson of this crime. You must have proof to accuse a respectable professional man of such a thing." You review what you know, trying to put the case in good order.
• *If you checked Clue I,* ***turn to 248.***
• *Otherwise,* ***turn to 255.***

238

You have no idea why the thief dropped the eagle into the chair. He certainly took a risk doing it — the eagle might have been damaged, or could have fallen to the floor with a crash! ***Turn to 106.***

239

Declining the Colonel's invitation, you return to the drawing room and pick up your book again. *Turn to 126.*

240

You examine the window sill and frame as carefully as you can, but find no clues which would identify the intruder. There is a little dirt on the sill, but must have come from the ground just below the window. Frustrated, you close the window and look over the rest of the room. *Turn to 152.*

241

"I also know that Grayson is a dead shot," you continue. "And a man would have to be a superb marksman to be able to wound Mortimer only slightly from that distance. I think the graze across the back of the neck was a precise shot, designed to wound Mortimer, not kill him."

"Very interesting," Holmes says, "you have built something of a case. Do you have other evidence?"

- If you checked Clues G and H, *turn to 271.*
- If you checked either Clue G or H, *turn to 279.*
- Otherwise, *turn to 604.*

242

You slip the piece of metal into the lock and wriggle it carefully. You frown and wriggle it again, adjusting it one more time and jabbing it very carefully inside the padlock, but you cannot open it. But could a more skilled man open the lock with the metal? *Turn to 442.*

243

"Where did that ladder come from?" you ask Colonel Dunlop.

"Most libraries do not have shelves as high as mine," Dunlop answers, pointing up. "We need the ladder to reach the upper shelves. Perhaps I should have put it somewhere else for the weekend, but it has been over there in the corner." He makes a vague gesture. ***Turn to 172.***

244

You cannot locate any sign of the solicitor's trail. Without such a clue, it is silly to try to follow him, and you dejectedly return to the house. Once more you pick up your book and return to its stories of past wars, still wondering about Grayson and his hike through the woods. ***Turn to 160.***

245

The spinning apple is too much for Watson and Snead, but to your surprise, you manage to drill one through the middle. While you stand smiling and dumbstruck at your luck, Grayson shatters his apple with a quick shot. You will have to survive another of Redruth's devices! The last challenge defeats you. Redruth sends a half-crown piece spinning high into the air, and you shoot so desperately that you have no idea whether or not you came close to the coin. To your amazement, Grayson's shot sends the coin flying with a ping. He laughs at his luck as everyone congratulates him on his victory. But you are not at all certain that luck had much to do with his win; Grayson is a dead shot. With shouts of "I am famished!" and much good-natured ribbing, your companions turn their thoughts to lunch. *Check Clue I. **Turn to 345.***

"What kind of outings will we have this weekend?" you ask Captain Leaf.

"Oh, a great variety of activity indeed!" Leaf says cheerfully. "You are a difficult man to please if you don't enjoy them. Tomorrow, we shall have a shooting contest for everyone, both men and women. Saturday, we shall test what every one of us can do on horseback, and probably cap our ride with a steeplechase, if we can't think of something even more exciting. But Sunday will be the best of all."

"What happens on Sunday?" you ask.

"We shall recreate one of the proudest moments in the history of the battery, sir. Just days before the battle of Waterloo, two officers — Mortimer and Snead — of the Yorkshire Lights fought a duel. It seems that one refused to allow the other man to marry his sister. They faced each other with pistols; after Lieutenant Mortimer missed, Lieutenant Snead fired wide intentionally. Some of the observers doubted the sincerity of the handshake after the duel; however, at Waterloo each man saved the other's life." Almost overcome by emotion, the Captain pauses to collect himself before continuing. "Not that it did them much good, because they were both mortally wounded before the day was done. Yet their colleagues were astonished by the honour of their actions. So every year we recreate the duel, with blanks in the guns, of course."

At this point Watson rescues you from the Captain, who then hunts a new victim to verbally overwhelm. *Check Clue D.* **Turn to 263.**

247

Holmes listens carefully to your story, then shakes his head. "You have no physical evidence indicating who shot Mortimer," he says. "You therefore must examine possible motives for the shooting."

"Perhaps I should suggest possible motives," Watson says, "and you two can decide whether there is any merit in what I suggest."

"Go ahead, Watson," Holmes says, settling himself to listen.

"First, there are the innocent explanations," Watson says. "Could the shot have been an accident, someone hunting deep in the woods and firing a shot which strayed further than he could imagine? Or perhaps some part of the gun wounded Mortimer, eh?"

Holmes scowls, unamused by the good doctor's ideas. "Watson, you are an unchanging star in the universe. You always find the least plausible answer to any question I pose."

You watch Dr. Watson formulate a defense which Mr. Holmes cuts off. "For a random shot to have been fired at the same instant as Snead's is beyond the bounds of coincidence," the detective concludes. "I believe that someone would have noticed had a piece of the gun broken free. Try again, my good fellow."

Watson takes a deep breath. "It is my duty to provide you with a little amusement, Holmes. Very well, perhaps our friend should choose among the following: Mortimer was shot because someone did not like him, because someone did not like Snead, or perhaps because someone wished to forestall the Snead-Mortimer wedding. The older Mortimers jumped at the chance to break the engagement when they thought Snead the guilty party."

Holmes glances at you; your body temperature rises. "Which motive seems likely to you?" he asks. "Then we shall discuss the logic of your choice."

- *If you choose hatred for Mortimer, **turn to 559.***
- *If you choose hatred for Snead, **turn to 366.***
- *If you choose breaking up the marriage, **turn to 156.***

248

"Grayson is a dead shot," you conclude. "Such skill is necessary to commit this crime."

"Perhaps it is," Holmes replies, "but I have heard very little evidence yet. Do you have any real evidence?" ***Turn to 281.***

249

You recall the greyish mud you found on the ladder and realize that some of it probably remains on the thief's shoes. Snead's shoes lie on the floor by his bed.

- *If you examine his shoes, **turn to 176.***
- *Otherwise, **turn to 566.***

250

"Grayson, the solicitor, was the hidden marksman," you announce.

"So you say," Holmes replies as he fills his pipe. "Do you have any evidence?"

• *If you checked Clue Q,* **turn to 594.**
• *Otherwise:*
  • *If you checked Deduction 12,* **turn to 229.**
  • *If not,* **turn to 237.**

251

You consider asking Leaf what he means by 'benefits', but let the reference pass. With the Captain, one always faces the danger of being trapped by an endless anecdote. Before you can ask Leaf anything else, Grayson and the elder Mr. Mortimer drift by and sample the brandy.

• *If you have not checked Decision 15 and wish to talk to Colonel Dunlop,* **turn to 440.**
• *If you have not checked Decision 16 and wish to talk to Dr. Cunningham,* **turn to 204.**
• *If you have completed the interviews,* **turn to 349.**

252

You can think of no way to continue your pursuit of Grayson; at least the outing proved to be more an exercise of your skills than a serious chase. At a few minutes before noon, you return to the house and resume your reading. *Turn to 160.*

253

You follow the path, which leads towards Gunston, but there are no footprints in its hard surface. Just as you are about to give up, you find a broken branch indicating that someone left the path. You follow the only route through the woods from that spot, and in the bottom of a small stream, you find one footprint. The slow-moving water has not erased it yet, but you know that the mark will soon be washed away. How can you measure the footprint? *Pick a number and add your Scholarship bonus:*

• *If 2-7,* **turn to 577.**
• *If 8-12,* **turn to 557.**

254

"Let us begin with the theft of the eagle," Holmes says, reaching for a cigarette. "We can deal with the shooting later."
• *If you checked Decision 21,* ***turn to 115.***
• *Otherwise,* ***turn to 460.***

255

"Come, come," the Colonel says, scolding you. "Did you pick the man's name out of the air?"

"Surely you have some evidence," Holmes says quietly. You try to marshall your thoughts under their imposing stares.
• *If you checked Clue G and Clue H,* ***turn to 287.***
• *Otherwise,* ***turn to 593.***

256

After the meal, there is still time before the hour set for the exchange of shots: five minutes past noon. The various guests form themselves into little groups, with the duellists standing alone, growing nervous in spite of the empty guns. The tension in the air is almost palpable. ***Turn to 381.***

257

You study the dumbwaiter ropes, and suddenly you understand why they will no longer work. Someone has used a bit of wire to tie them together. ***Turn to 356.***

258

"Now, what was it you wanted me to explain?" Leaf asks. "The details of our service in Afghanistan, or the mess the paper-pushers made when we drew coast-defense duty during the Crimean War?"

You try to think of the better question to ask.
• *If you ask about anyone benefiting from the breakup up the Mortimer-Snead engagement,* ***turn to 497.***
• *If you ask what will happen as a result of the wedding,* ***turn to 597.***

259

You walk to the library door and look up at the mantle. As you were certain it would be, the eagle remains perched in place. Satisfied but nervous, you return to your chair. *Check Decision 18.* **Turn to 339.**

260

You consider the evidence you have, deciding which clue to discuss first.

• *If you checked Clue U,* **turn to 208.**
• *Otherwise,* **turn to 213.**

261

"But tell me," Watson asks insistently, "what potential gain could lead a respected solicitor even to consider so risky and disgraceful an undertaking? The man would throw away everything he has worked for all his life in one foolish and doomed gesture." You carefully consider Watson's probing question. *Pick a number and add your Scholarship bonus:*
• *If 2-7,* **turn to 178.**
• *If 8-12,* **turn to 602.**

262

You search your mind for the proper question, then say: "It's a pleasure to meet a loyal Canadian, Mr. Snead, but it must be a strange path that led you here today."

He looks a little surprised, then smiles. "Aye, I've been very lucky, friend," he laughs, covering a mouthful of ugly teeth. "I came across on business, with letters of introduction to the Colonel. It so happens that my great grandfather served in the Yorkshire Lights at Waterloo, and the Colonel insisted that I come to the reunion, to celebrate the seventy-fifth anniversary of the battle. And by even greater good fortune, he introduced me to Susan, who has decided to marry me and to return to my home in Canada." Snead playfully raises a toast to his fiance, who smiles in return. "In just two weeks we shall be married, and in three weeks, our ship sails for my homeland." The delighted bridegroom-to-be winks playfully at Miss Mortimer, who blushes and lowers her head.
• *If you ask further questions of Snead,* **turn to 582.**
• *Otherwise,* **turn to 436.**

After talking to Leaf, you wander out in the hallway, where a strange spectacle greets your eyes. Lieutenant Mortimer enters through the French windows of the drawing room, dragging a smaller, crudely-dressed man behind him.

"What's this, Mortimer?" the Colonel asks in a surprised voice. "Why, it's Badger Phillips. What have you been up to, Badger?" he asks the smaller man.

"Nothing, guv," the little man answers quickly, "I ain't been up to a thing, sir; you know I wouldn't do anything wrong."

"I caught this fellow setting snares in your woods, sir," Mortimer says. "I knew you wouldn't allow that."

"And what was he doing in the woods 'imself?" Phillips asks.

"Oh, be quiet, both of you," the Colonel says, examining both men warily. "Thank you, Mortimer; I appreciate your concern. You, Badger, shall appear before me Tuesday morning at ten, and I shall decide then to do about this offense." As the little scene breaks up, you turn to go upstairs. Watson joins you. ***Turn to 338.***

264

Miss Dunlop seems to consider the question for a long moment. "I left the bedroom as soon as I saw that Dr. Cunningham had the situation under control and did not require my help. I needed to go upstairs and change, as my shoes and clothes were quite muddy. But I hesitated a moment as I left John's room, for I saw Robert Snead outside the library, just standing there. Then he went upstairs, and I followed a minute later." *Check Clue BB. Pick a number* and *add your Intuition Bonus:*

- *If 2-7, turn to 483.*
- *If 8-12, turn to 419.*

265

You carefully work at the lock, and soon you feel movement. The knob turns freely in your hand, but the door does not open. You remember that it is secured inside by bolts. You test it and find that the door will not move when you shake it. You cannot find any way to release the bolts. *Pick a number* and *add your Intuition bonus:*

- *If 2-7, turn to 223.*
- *If 8-12, turn to 387.*

266

You examine the lock and the bolts again. Recalling some of what Holmes has taught you about locks (and deducing from the position of the bolts it would have been impossible for someone to have secured them from the other side), you find yourself one step closer to solving the puzzle. *Turn to 567.*

267

When you carefully think through what happened, you recall that Miss Dunlop had to be the one who ran through the mud, although you cannot imagine why the Colonel's niece would rob him. But she was the only person who went back to the house by herself, so that no one would have seen her run through the mud. Also, when she hurried to the house to get help for the wounded Mortimer, she would have followed the most direct path and not worried about the mud. *Check Deduction 22. Turn to 598.*

268

"What do you mean about Mr. Snead?" you ask Mr. Foxx. "He seems a pleasant fellow."

"Oh, absolutely wonderful," Foxx agrees sarcastically, then adding: "He is quick to seize opportunities, sometimes before they are available. You perhaps do not know that Miss Mortimer was once my fiance. We had separated temporarily over a simple misunderstanding, and before I could take steps to rectify matters, that Canadian sharp had slipped into my slippers and robe, so to speak."

"The girl is free to choose her destiny, Hunter; the Middle Ages have ended," the Colonel comments. "Don't blame Snead because you were fool enough to let her go."

"Perhaps," Foxx snaps, "but I did not refuse to take my position in the duel, Colonel. You took that from me."

"Now, Hunter," the Colonel says, trying to mollify the angry fellow, "I explained that to you. You can be one of the duelists every other year for the next fifty, if you so desire. This is Snead's only opportunity, and it is particularly appropriate on the seventy-fifth anniversary of the original duel. I have agreed to allow you the honor of loading the pistols on Friday; considering the tradition governing the re-creation, that action may be a more important task than firing a gun." Foxx growls something barely audible but does not argue openly with the Colonel. ***Pick a number*** and *add your Intuition bonus:*

• *If 2-6,* ***turn to 471.***
• *If 7-12,* ***turn to 179.***

269

There is so much talk at dinner (and the laughter all but constant) that you cannot pinpoint the source of the tension that you sensed. Everyone seems to eagerly anticipate tomorrow's re-creation of the duel, although Colonel Dunlop's comments seem a bit distracted and ominous. *Turn to 302.*

270

"If he was not shot from hatred," Watson suggests, "then one of the other two motives must be valid. Unless you are hiding something, Holmes," he adds, casting a suspicious look at his friend.

"I would say that one of the other reasons is probably valid," Holmes replies calmly. Then he asks you: "Which seems more likely to you?"

• *If you name hatred for Snead, turn to 366.*
• *If you name preventing the wedding, turn to 156.*

271

"The first night I was here," you reveal, "I surprised a man handling the duelling pistols in the gun room. From his size and some hairs I found, I am certain that the intruder was Thomas Grayson. He must have had some evil plan in mind to look at the pistols late at night."

Holmes considers the evidence, then says: "While you have little evidence to convict the man, I think you have found substantial evidence to suspect Grayson. Good work." *Turn to 604.*

272

You turn around, carefully examining the study, wondering what to do now that you are here. Your after-dark expedition seems sillier now than it did when you first discussed it with Watson.

• *If you checked Decision 7, turn to 521.*
• *Otherwise, turn to 560.*

Subdued by the shooting, you find that everyone at Eagle Towers has scattered to different parts of the house after dinner. This scattering should enable you to talk with the people who might know something useful without attracting undue attention. Snead, John Mortimer and Susan Mortimer are in John's bedroom, talking quietly.

• *If you talk to the Mortimers and Snead, **turn to 376.***
• *If you talk to Colonel Dunlop, **turn to 440.***
• *If you talk to Dr. Cunningham, **turn to 204.***
• *If you talk to Captain Leaf, **turn to 532.***

274

Looking more carefully, you see a branch of a bush move against the breeze. Someone is hiding there! You start to say something, then change your mind. You do not have any evidence that the watcher has any ill intentions. Telling the others could postpone the duel, and if you delayed it for a false alarm, Colonel Dunlop would probably drive you off with a horsewhip. Probably nothing will come of it. *Check Clue S. Turn to 320.*

275

You wonder if some outsider might have slipped through the drawing room and taken the eagle. You go outside and look around, and see that Redruth, the aging, wizened groundskeeper, is working near the end of the house.

"Have you been here all morning?" you ask Redruth.

"Aye, sir, that I have," the groundskeeper answers. "Leastways I've been here since ten o'clock, trying to fill in a bad spot in the gardens."

"Has anyone come in the house through the drawing room?" you ask.

"No, no one at all," he answers. "Nor gone out except for Mr. Harris." You thank him and return to the library. No outsider stole the eagle, it seems. *Turn to 473.*

"Someone fired from the woods! I saw smoke!" you shout, pointing toward the bushes.

Watson looks to where you are pointing and adds his cry to yours. "I saw a little smoke there, gentlemen," he cries, though the breeze has dispersed it. "Hurry! We must catch the bounder!"

As Watson tends the fallen man, Foxx, Dunlop and Snead join you and run across the clearing. The sniper is gone by the time you reach the bushes, and you restrain the others so that they will not wipe out any footprints. Slowly, you enter the bushes, searching the ground for clues. *Turn to 404.*

277

Soon Beach strikes the gong in the hallway, and everyone files into the dining room for dinner. The dinner reflects this luxurious life at its best. Both ladies are dressed in beautiful silk gowns, set off by jeweled necklaces and bracelets. The gentlemen wear either formal clothes or military dress uniforms.

When everyone is seated, Beach and his staff bring in the first course. The talk around the table quickly grows lively, with jokes about the recreated duel to be acted out on the morrow. In spite of the lively talk and course after course of excellent food, you sense an undercurrent of tension, although you cannot discern its source. *Pick a number* and add your Intuition bonus:

• If 2-7, *turn to 269.*
• If 8-12, *turn to 135.*

278

You draw near to the intruder and see that he is handling the case of old duelling pistols the Colonel showed you the afternoon before. What interest could these guns have? *Check Clue F.* ***Turn to 133.***

279

"My evidence is hardly impressive," you say, "but on the first night I was here, I surprised someone in the gun room, examining the duelling pistols. I think Grayson was the man."

"Little that you offer is impressive," Holmes replies, "but assembled, the facts form a reasonable proof that Grayson shot Mortimer. You could have done worse." ***Turn to 604.***

280

You display considerable skill at rock-throwing. In the midst of a tossing a barrage of stones that must have frightened every animal for miles around, you hit the largest pan with your first toss and the second biggest after one miss. Dr. Cunningham is the only other contestant to hit the third pan. Now the competition grows more serious. You draw a deep breath before throwing at the smallest pan, your tension increasing when the doctor hits it on his first attempt.

"You must hit it to remain competitive," Miss Dunlop announces. You throw and are pleased to hear a clang. You take your second throw first, and the doctor matches your success.

"Down to the last throw," Miss Dunlop announces, clearly impressed. "What a pair of titans! The Doctor is first," she adds.

With the easy motion he has used the entire contest, the doctor makes the pan chime like a church bell. You now feel some pressure, and your arm seems to weigh ten stone. Your last effort hits the rope above the pan, but there is no doubt in anyone's mind: it's a miss. The doctor has won!

You are the first to congratulate him. Then the merry group fords the stream and follows a trail through the woods on the other side. ***Turn to 431.***

281

You desperately strive to recall evidence while the others watch.

- *If you checked Clue G or Clue H,* ***turn to 282.***
- *Otherwise,* ***turn to 288.***

282

"The first night I was here," you say, "I surprised someone in the gun room, looking at the duelling pistols. I think it was Grayson." Taking a breath, you outline the evidence.

Holmes listens carefully. "You have some proof," he says finally, "though I would like to see more concrete evidence." ***Turn to 604.***

283

In spite of your efforts to direct the conversation, the Captain babbles on in a genial monologue. Trapped in the corner, you realize that you will not be able to investigate anything else this evening. ***Turn to 263.***

284

The second target is quite large, but your nerves get the best of you, and you miss. You are embarassed, but the ladies hurriedly reassure you. "Don't worry," Miss Dunlop cries, "it could have happened to anyone. We would appreciate it if you would help Redruth choose and set up targets for the following shots." You readily agree and in a matter of minutes, find Redruth an imaginitive companion. As the competition continues, he uses such things as empty cans, apples and branches to thin out the contestants. You come up with one or two bright ideas that help to make the targets more difficult to hit. *Pick a number* and add your *Observation bonus:*

• *If 2-7, turn to 321.*
• *If 8-12, turn to 206.*

285

Foxx has a comfortable room facing the east, with heavy curtains to protect a guest's slumber from the early sun. The bed is perfectly made. You see two possible hiding places — a heavy wooden dresser and a large wardrobe. Searching both of them, you find nothing suspicious. You stand in the center of the room and look around again. *Pick a number and add your Observation bonus:*

• *If 2-6, turn to 442.*
• *If 7-12, turn to 518.*

286

With a start you realize that the padlock on the trunk is virtually identical to the one that protected the eagle. You wonder whether Snead's key might work in the padlock from the library.

• *If you try the key, turn to 357.*
• *Otherwise, turn to 107.*

287

"The first night I was here," you say, "I surprised an intruder in the gun room, looking at the duelling pistols. From his size and some hairs I found, the intruder must have been Grayson. If he waited until two in the morning to look at the pistols, he must have had some questionable reason to be there." *Turn to 288.*

288

"You have uncovered some evidence that points towards Grayson," Holmes says. "You have not proved your charge, however. You must do better in the future. Or have you established a motive that makes physical proof almost irrelevant?" Perhaps you should try to investigate the case again.
• *If you want to explain the motive, turn to 298.*
• *If you ask Holmes to explain it, turn to 290.*
• *If you want to investigate the case again, turn to the Prologue.*

289

"I am certain that the eagle is hidden in the dumbwaiter," you mutter, staring at the ropes.

"And so it is," Holmes answers. He reaches into the dumbwaiter and unwraps a piece of wire that binds the ropes together. When he works them, the tray descends into sight, and the eagle rests upon it!

"I say!" cries the Colonel, delighted. He reaches for the treasured standard before you move to help. *Turn to 589.*

290

"Please explain, Mr. Holmes," you say, a little bitterly. "I am certain that you have uncovered all relevant evidence."

"As it happens, I have established the proof," asserts Holmes. "First, Grayson is a crack shot, a skill necessary to carry out this crime. I also found physical evidence of his crime. His shot left a burn mark on some leaves, and I was able to follow his trail from there. While he did not leave any identifiable footprints, the trail led towards Gunston. I saw Grayson arrive at the town at a time that would fit perfectly with the timing of the shooting." *Turn to 303.*

"It's an easy life to grow accustomed to," Harris laughs, displaying a nice set of teeth. He is a handsome fellow. "I should press my advantages if I were you, sir — perhaps you shall own such a house one day. Heed this advice: when others give you an opportunity to make a profit, do not let their loss bother you. All the money one makes must come out of someone else's pocket, you know."

"I don't quite understand, sir," you say in a questioning voice.

"Oh, I am certain that you do," he replies, eyeing you slyly. "If you learn that the favorite in a horse race is ill, would you tell that to all the people betting on him, or would you take advantage of the information and wager on another horse? If you held an unbeatable hand at poker, would you advise the poor fool seated next to you drop out just as he is about to wager against you? You would not! Nor would you sacrifice a good business advantage, not at any cost!" You wonder how Harris earns a living when he isn't gambling. *Check Deduction 5*. **Turn to 502.**

"What are you doing here?" you demand. With a startled gasp, the stranger closes his lamp and dives for an open window. Before you can move, he is gone! Looking out the window, you see no sign of the intruder. You could not tell what he was doing, but wonder if he left any clue to his identity. **Turn to 361.**

"What is so odd about it, Captain Leaf?" you ask. "I admit irony in it. The first duel was fought because such a wedding was squashed, and now the re-enactment has blocked the wedding."

"Aye, you have touched it there, lad," he answers, and launches into a tale of an Indian wedding that turned into a small war. At least the old man's story helps to pass the time as you wait for Mr. Holmes. **Turn to 403.**

294

"Beach stole the eagle," you boldly assert. "He took advantage of the confusion that filled the house after Miss Dunlop brought news of the shooting." The other three men stare at you in amazement. "An incredible deduction!" Holmes comments, "And very daring, when you lack a single piece of evidence to support it."

"Am I wrong?" you ask timidly.

"Absolutely incorrect!" Holmes replies, puffing at a cigarette. "If Beach, who seems a most honest fellow at any rate, wished to steal something from his master's house, he would plan the theft in advance. He has too much to lose to commit any but the most carefully- planned crime. This was not such a deed." *Turn to 540.*

295

In spite of his efforts, you outmaneuver the poacher. Finally, you lock his arm behind his back and lean your weight into the hold. Phillips gasps in pain, then begs: "Please, sir, let go! I'll tell you what you want to know."

You rise slowly, watching the man, but all the fight has gone out of him. He sits up, but does not try to stand, and holds his sore arm with the other hand. *Turn to 195.*

296

In spite of your care, you step onto a dry branch, hidden by the grass. It snaps with a noise that seems louder than a gunshot, in the still of the evening. Without stopping to look, the intruder takes off running along the edge of the woods. You cannot see his face, and he vanishes before you can react and pursue him. *Turn to 413.*

"I think that an outsider slipped in and stole the eagle," you say. "The Colonel should begin by questioning that poacher, Badger Phillips."

"Indeed I shall," the Colonel says eagerly, rising to his feet.

"Do not waste your time," Holmes interposes coldly. The Colonel slowly takes his seat. "No outsider could have touched the golden bird. Redruth the groundskeeper was outside watching all morning, while he worked in the garden near the drawing room. It would be absolute folly for an outsider to attempt such a crime in the middle of the day. There were too many people here." *Turn to 540.*

"But I do know Grayson's motive," you insist. "That is why I accused him."

"Then tell us," Holmes urges.

- *If you checked Clue L and either Clue K or N,*
 turn to 299.
- *If you checked Clue L but not Clue K or N, turn to 301.*
- *Otherwise, turn to 572.*

"I have learned that Grayson needed money," you begin, "money to continue operation of his company. He was trustee for an estate that would have paid a large sum to Snead and Miss Mortimer when they wed. I feel certain that he could not afford to pay the money, probably because it was invested in his business. He knew that if Snead appeared to shoot Mortimer, it would lead to the cancellation of the wedding. As Snead is leaving the country in a few weeks, there would be no chance for a reconciliation."

"Well done," Holmes says quietly, "you are learning your trade well." The other men discuss the case in more detail, as you sit back and savor the compliment. But already you are turning your thoughts to the future. What challenges will your next case bring? The End

300

As you stand and think, Watson comes out of the water closet. "I have finished searching the other rooms for the eagle," he says, scratching his head. "There is no sign of it anywhere. I wonder where that thing can be," he adds. Wondering the same thing, you thank him, and the two of you return downstairs. *Turn to 579.*

301

You explain that Grayson controls a trust, the capital of which will be paid to Snead and Miss Mortimer upon their marriage. "But that in itself is no reason for the shooting," Holmes comments. "There is no evidence that Grayson has abused his trust."

"Then why did he shoot Mortimer?" Watson asks.

"He could not afford to pay the cash of the trust to the young couple," Holmes answers. "Therefore, he shot Mortimer in a way that would shift the blame to Snead, thus preventing the wedding." As Holmes, Watson and the Colonel discuss the case, you sit back and try to see where you went wrong. You resolve that in your next case, you will cast a keener eye on suspects and clues. The End

302

Finally, the feast comes to an end. It seems a long time before you can get your legs under you and rise to your feet.

Gradually the dinner party breaks up. The Colonel, Foxx and Jackson sit long over the port, each getting comfortably drunk. Harris takes Miss Dunlop out for a walk. The Mortimers challenge Snead and Grayson to a game of whist. Seeing you standing alone for a moment, Dr. Watson urges you to join him, Captain Leaf, and Dr. Cunningham in a game of billiards.

• *If you join the billiards game, turn to 422.*
• *If you go outside for a walk, turn to 449.*
• *If you go into the library to read, turn to 174.*

"But why did Grayson shoot Mortimer?" Watson demands.

"I learned the answer to that question while pursuing my own research in Gunston," replies Holmes, crushing his cigarette in an ashtray at his side. "I found an old will and trust, which stipulate that a large sum of money will be given to Mr. Snead and Miss Mortimer when they wed. Our friend Grayson is sole trustee. I am certain that he has already committed the money to his current project, the Whitby and York Railway. If Grayson were forced to pay out the money from the estate, it would ruin him and sink his company as well. The railway is quite short of cash. Grayson knew that if it appeared that Snead shot Mortimer, the wedding would no doubt be cancelled."

"An amazing scheme," Watson says thoughtfully. "The scoundrel was lucky, crack shot or not, that he did not wound Mortimer seriously."

You and the Colonel agree. "I will deal with this matter, Mr. Holmes," the Colonel says. "Please stay here as my guest."

The next day and evening fly by, marked by the happiness of the two couples planning their weddings. Of course, Thomas Grayson leaves hurriedly the next morning.

On the return trip to London, you try to listen to Holmes as he discusses the jewel theft in Cornwall, but your mind runs to a different question: when will you be able to try your hand at another puzzling case? The End

"I have no idea why Grayson would shoot you, Lieutenant Mortimer," you admit, "nor even any idea why he would want to commit a crime. He seems to be an ordinary, honest man."

"I do not know if this is the cause of his action," Jackson says, "but I know that he is desperately short of cash. He has all his funds tied up in the Whitby and York railway. But I do not know how he would get the money by shooting at Mortimer."

• If you checked Clue L, **turn to 364.**
• Otherwise, **turn to 112.**

305

Curious, you stick your head out the door and glance down the hall. Miss Mortimer stands by the door leading into the library, though you cannot tell what she is doing. At the sound of your door opening, she turns away and goes downstairs. You and Watson finish dressing and start downstairs. Passing the library door, you stop to look at it, wondering if Miss Mortimer might have done something to it. *Check Clue J. **Pick a number** and add your Observation bonus:*

• If 2-7, **turn to 467.**
• If 8-12. **turn to 399.**

306

You study the bags, then answer: "They must be yours, Mr. Holmes. I recognize the customs marks of several countries which you have visited in the course of your investigations. Cousin John has not left England since his marriage."

"Very good," Holmes says quietly. "Now let me tell you why I sent for you." **Turn to 317.**

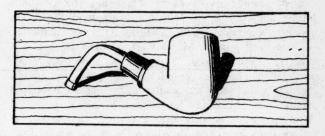

307

"One of the servants stole the eagle," you suggest. "Sharp questioning of them will probably wring a confession from the guilty party."

"No, no!" Holmes snaps, very perturbed. "There is no evidence to suggest that such a charge is true. 'One of the servants' indeed! You should be ashamed to make such a charge!" Turn **to 540.**

Oppressed by the heat of the house and anxious to see a little more of the beautifully-landscaped grounds, you wander outside through the French windows and walk across the yard. You notice Harris and Miss Dunlop walking around toward the back of the house, so you turn towards the front.

Just outside the front door, you encounter Lieutenant Mortimer, who also seems to be enjoying the night air. You join him and wander about the grounds, chatting. You try to get him to comment about the events of the weekend and his sister's wedding. ***Pick a number*** *and add your Communication bonus:*

• *If 2-6,* ***turn to 314.***
• *If 7-12,* ***turn to 469.***

Breakfast is the kind of meal one expects at a country mansion. Platters of bacon, eggs, sausage and kippers cover a sideboard, flanked by silver pots of coffee and tea. Baskets of fresh bread and buns cover another table top. The guests talk little as they devote their attention to the food. Finally, as appetites begin to wane, the talk turns to the day's activities.

"You must join us, Mister Hurley," Miss Dunlop says eagerly, addressing you. "Everyone can participate today, whatever their abilities. We will walk through the grounds this morning and observe the beauties of my uncle's house and grounds, and engage in a few contests of skill as we walk." After a pause, the lady addresses everyone. "No one dares to refuse, does he?" The guests hastily assure her of their participation. The veterans, Captain Leaf and Colonel Dunlop, lead the way once breakfast is finished. The Dunlops lead you through the grounds, proudly showing and describing many beautiful glens and sparkling brooks, until you come to a wide stream with rocks lining its banks. Oddly, several pans of different sizes are tied to branches of trees on the other side of the water.

"Now for a test of skill," Miss Dunlop laughs, signaling for the party to stop. "This will be easy," she says, nodding toward the far banks. "There are plenty of rocks, and all one must do is hit those pans. We begin with the biggest pan, and each of us throws three stones. Anyone who misses all three is eliminated. Then we move to the next smaller pan, and continue until only one of us remains." Eagerly, Captain Leaf bends and tosses a round stone into the bushes well to the right of the target. The others join in, and you await your turn. ***Pick a number*** and add your *Athletics* bonus:

• *If 2-6,* ***turn to 377.***
• *If 7-11,* ***turn to 280.***
• *If 12,* ***turn to 342.***

310

Certain that he has the attention of everyone, Holmes dramatically opens the dumbwaiter door in the library.

"It cannot be there," the Colonel argues. "It does not work!" Holmes tugs at the ropes, but they do not move. He looks at them more closely, then unwraps a bit of wire that held the ropes together. After this, the ropes function perfectly, and with a squeak, the tray comes into sight. Perched upon it is the magnificent golden eagle! ***Turn to 589.***

311

"I have seen him do nothing suspicious," you admit, "but I harbor some doubts about the fellow. I have tried to discover how he makes his living; he seems to be quite evasive about it. From his comments, I am not certain that he garners an income in an honest manner. However, I too hope he is innocent — it would hurt Miss Dunlop deeply if the fellow proved to be a cad." *Turn to 193.*

312

You think of two ways to set an alarm in the library. First, you might attach a thread to the eagle, the thread connecting to a small bell in your room, so that you will know if anyone touches the jeweled bird. Or you might set some heavy objects on the edge of the mantle so that anyone tampering with the bird will knock them over.

- If you rig the thread and small bell, *turn to 391.*
- If you set the trap to make a noise, *turn to 101.*
- If you decide not to set a trap, *turn to 405.*

313

Your pursuit of Grayson has become a challenge, and you start running through the woods, hoping to intercept him and continue your pursuit. *Pick a number and add your Athletics bonus:*

- If 2-9, *turn to 379.*
- If 10-12, *turn to 445.*

314

Mortimer seems anxious to control the flow of conversation and talks about the pleasures of a country weekend such as this. "It is a nice combination, sir," he says, "the luxuries of a fine house combined with various tests of strength and skill. You will be surprised at how quickly the weekend races by." *Turn to 210.*

315

You continue to talk to Jackson and Grayson, and after covering the shooting match, Grayson turns his eye to the eagle. "Have you ever seen the like?" he asks you.

"Oh no," you reply. "What a magnificent work of art. It is a shame that it is locked away so much of the time."

"It is a necessary precaution," says Grayson. "Aside from the value of the eagle as a treasure and a work of art, the gold and jewels by themselves are worth more than ten thousand pounds. I helped the Colonel arrange to insure it." *Check Deduction 4. **Turn to 128.***

316

Your curiosity gets the best of any restraints you might have. You carefully twist the wire free from the ropes, then lower the dumbwaiter back in place. When the shelf comes into sight, it carries a golden passenger! You have found the eagle!

Slapping you on the back and almost crowing with delight, the colonel helps you to remove the eagle and carry it to his study. "Well done, my boy, well done!" the Colonel cries, puffing as he carries one end of the magnificent standard. "How can you possibly have found such an unlikely hiding place?" the Colonel asks, clearly overwhelmed by your insight. "You shall always be a hero in this house, I promise you!"

Once in the study, the Colonel locks the eagle in his large safe. Catching your breath, you are pleased to have recovered the stolen treasure, but you still have not been able to identify the thief. "I must continue my investigation!" you tell your grateful host, who nods in agreement. *Check Decision 21. **Turn to 224.***

"I have been asked to investigate recent jewel thefts in Devon and Cornwall," Holmes explains. "Concurrently, another gentleman has asked for my assistance in protecting a great treasure. As I am otherwise engaged, you must go in my place. Fortunately, Watson has also been invited, and you may travel with him without arousing comment. Watson will enjoy your company, as his good wife is visiting a sick friend in Sussex."

"What am I to do?" you inquire. "Is there reason to suspect another theft?"

"I hesitate to comment without further evidence," Holmes answers, raising a long finger as he pauses to listen. "A cab downstairs — that will be Colonel Dunlop." Mrs. Hudson escorts the Colonel to Holmes' door, and the portly, middle-aged gentleman is soon seated in a comfortable chair, a glass of brandy in his hand.

"Is this the substitute you have arranged?" the stout military man asks, nodding toward you. "He looks quite young."

"He should fool any potential thief, then," Holmes replies, "if he is willing to accept the work. Perhaps you would be so kind as to explain your needs to young Mr. Hurley."

The Colonel frowns. "I have retired from the army," he begins, "and now live at Eagle Towers, near Gunston in Yorkshire. Among the units I have had the honour of commanding was the Yorkshire Light Artillery, a reserve unit with a proud history going back to Wellington's day. Every year, in the summer, I invite those men who have a connection with the unit to visit my home, to keep alive its tradition and glory, until the day that the unit may be activated again. During that brief annual period, the greatest of the Yorkshire Light's trophies is on display at my library."

"What trophy?" you ask, scribbling a few notes.

The Colonel takes a breath, perhaps bored. "A jeweled golden eagle, a foot high; it's priceless! For their courageous actions at the battle of Vittoria, where they helped the Highlanders capture a French Eagle, Wellington allowed the Yorkshire Lights to add an eagle to the battery's honours. The officers ordered it made from gold and jewels captured from a French baggage train."

"Why do you fear its theft?" you ask. "Have you invited suspicious guests to the reunion?"

"I cannot be certain," he answers, groping for the correct phrase, "but these terrible incidents must give any man pause. In addition to the caution expected of anyone responsible for so valuable a treasure, it happens that my niece's fiance Harris will be one of the guests this weekend."

"Do you distrust him?" you ask.

"I do not actually distrust Harris," the Colonel insists, looking uncomfortable. "However, he was a guest at two other mansions where thefts occurred, and while he seems to be well-off, I cannot discern how he makes his money. There are one or two other guests whom I do not know well. I had already invited Dr. Watson, whom I met in Afghanistan, so you will cause no undue comment as an additional guest. And I must admit," the Colonel concludes, "I would just feel more comfortable if there were someone on the premises actively protecting the eagle. Mr. Holmes has recommended you, as he cannot come himself. I will pay you well."

"I accept the invitation," you answer at once. "When should we arrive?"

"The reunion begins tomorrow, Wednesday," the Colonel replies. "Take the morning train from King's Cross Station and change at South Riding, to the local line to Gunston. You should arrive in the middle of the afternoon. I must hurry to catch my own train," the Colonel adds, rising as he drains the glass of brandy. "I shall see you at Eagle Towers tomorrow afternoon." He nods to Holmes and Watson and leaves.

After the Colonel has gone, Watson asks Holmes: "Do you think there is any basis for his fears? He presented an interesting thesis to support his suspicions of his son-in-law to be."

Holmes smiles, perhaps amused at your cousin's tortured phrase. "I think you and your cousin will have a very pleasant weekend at the Colonel's expense," he says, "but I may be wrong. I have a complete list of the guests, and none seems a likely jewel thief to me. But the trip will do neither of you any harm. If I finish my own investigations quickly, I will come to Gunston myself. There are documents in the town hall that I should examine to prepare my monograph on early English charters. Good hunting!" In one smooth motion, Holmes picks up his bags and hurries down the stairs. His whistle quickly summons a hansom, and you hear him tell the cabman to take him to Paddington.

"I will pick you up at your lodgings in the morning," Doctor Watson says as you prepare to leave. He flips open the Bradshaw to confirm his memory. "Our train leaves at half-past seven, so be ready early."

Back at your quarters you pack and try to get to sleep early, but you find yourself too excited to rest. Your mind is ablaze with villainous scenarios! The next morning dawns overcast, but you are ready and waiting when Watson comes by in a growler. Neither of you speaks of the case until you are settled into your compartment on the train a half-hour later.

"I shall enjoy this weekend," Watson predicts, watching the passing of many nameless strangers in the station, "even if we have no adventures. Holmes however would detest such a weekend, unless he has an investigation in hand. He is a Londoner to the core of his being and has no love for any other place on earth."

"Has Holmes told you anything about the other jewel thefts?" you ask Watson, as the train jerks to a start and leaves the station. "What kind of theft might we be asked to stop?"

"Oh, you know Holmes," Watson answers obliquely, "he's never willing to say anything until he's examined the scene of the crime. But I have looked through the newspaper accounts and police reports that were sent to Holmes. The Bristol and Falmouth papers carried much longer accounts than the London dailies. Would you like me to summarize my notes?"

"Yes, tell me what you learned," you say, settling back to listen as suburban London rushes past your window.

Looking pleased, Watson pulls a bunch of papers from his pocket. "The first theft took place at a mansion owned by Lord Dodge, about ten miles outside Plymouth. At the time of the theft, he had a houseful of guests, plus servants, of course. There was a cry of "Fire!" one night after everyone had gone to bed, and all fled the house. The butler then found that someone had set ablaze a pile of wet straw in a back hall — it produced a good deal of smoke without doing much damage. The next morning, one of the ladies' discovered that her diamond-and- pearl necklace — worth ten thousand — was gone."

"Presumably, someone set fire to the straw to produce the smoke and then took advantage of the confusion to steal the necklace, which he must have known about," you mutter. "And the other theft?"

"That occurred at Tristram House, near Tintagil in Cornwall," replies Watson. "Again, there was a grand to-do, with as many as a dozen guests. They played cards very late one night, with everyone participating. When they retired to their rooms, one of the ladies screamed in fear. Others rushed to her room and discovered a ladder leaning against an open window. The lady's jewel case had been forced open, and some five thousand worth of rings and bracelets were gone. As the second theft followed the first by only a week, it created a major scandal."

"It seems as if the rogue is working his way west," you comment, reviewing the facts as your cousin has stated them.

"If the cad travels west from Cornwall, he'll be forced to commit the next theft on the high seas," Watson laughs. "But Holmes will see through him, even though they waited so long to invite him to investigate the case." As Watson talks further, you pause to contemplate the facts you have learned. *Pick a number and add your Intuition bonus:*
- If 2-7, **turn to 538.**
- If 8-12, **turn to 429.**

318

"I am not sure why Grayson shot him," you admit. "I know that Grayson needed money, but I do not understand how his case would be helped by shooting Mortimer."

"But I do," Holmes says, intently cleaning his pipe. You and Watson look at him, waiting for an explanation. After a pause, the great detective resumes speaking; you are struck by how professorial he can be. "This afternoon, I read a very strange old will at the local courthouse. Under its terms, a large sum of money is to be paid to Mr. Snead and Miss Mortimer when they wed. Grayson is the trustee; I know something of his affairs. He has undoubtedly tied that money up in his dubious enterprises, so that being forced to pay it out would be a financial disaster for him. I dislike all such wills," Holmes adds, frowning. "They are an invitation to dishonesty." He then begins to respond to Watson's demand for the whole story regarding his quick solution of the jewel thefts.

Though you try to listen, you find your thoughts drifting away, as you wonder what challenges and dangers your next investigation will bring. The End

319

Anyone hiding in the corner must be up to no good. If you were to approach him, the culprit might attack. It is neither wise nor necessary to take any chances now. *Turn to 393.*

320

In the interval before the duel, Leaf comes over to talk to you. "I doubt that anyone has given you the exact order of events," he says, "and I think you will enjoy matters more if you know what is scheduled to happen, when." You nod in thanks. "The men will stand ten paces apart," the Captain continues, squinting in the sun. "I will give them the word, 'Ready,' and then count to five. In the original duel, neither man could fire before the first count or after the last. In fact, Mortimer shot as the second called 'One!' while Snead shot wide at the count of 'Three!' Both gentlemen today have been briefed to fire their shots at the exact moment chosen by their Great-Grandfathers. You might find it amusing to see how close they come to the exact second."

The bell in a distant church tower chimes the hour — twelve o'clock! Captain Leaf consults his watch, signals for quiet, and summons the duellists. "Are you gentlemen certain that bloodshed must settle your dispute?" he asks.

Both men nod and mumble something that you cannot hear. Then Leaf spins a coin in the air, Snead calls heads, and Leaf announces that he has won the toss. The Captain picks up the pistols, trades them back and forth between his hands quickly, and offers them to Snead. The Canadian takes one, Mortimer accepts the other, and Dunlop and Jackson lead the combatants to their places. You glance at your watch — four minutes past noon. It is almost time!

Leaf gives his instructions as he told you he would. "I will say 'Ready!' and then count to five. You must shoot between the count of one and five."

- If you checked Clue S, **turn to 484.**
- Otherwise, **turn to 416.**

321

You find it is almost as pleasurable to set up the targets as it is to shoot at (and miss!) them. Several competitors continue the fierce but friendly struggle, but finally you come upon a way to find a winner. You and Redruth tie apples to strings, hang them from a tree limb, and then tell the last three shooters that they must cut the string. When Grayson cuts his apple down with his first shot, Watson and Snead stare helplessly at each other, then laugh and make their futile efforts. Everyone congratulates the clear winner, Grayson, for his luck and skill. *Turn to 345.*

322

"John," you say excitedly to Watson, "how could a shot fired by Snead have scraped the back of Mortimer's neck? Mortimer's side was pointed towards Snead, but his head was turned towards him to aim; thus, a shot fired by Snead could have scraped the side of his neck but not the back."

"My word," Watson mutters, "You are right. Why didn't I see that? Quiet, everyone," he cries, turning to the rest of the group. "My cousin has reached a startling conclusion. Mr. Snead could not have hit Lieutenant Mortimer in the back of his neck from where he was standing. Someone else must have fired at the same time, from another location." Watson points towards the woods, fifty yards away, where the puff of smoke arose. *Check Clue V. Turn to 456.*

323

These locks have not been broken by some heavy tool, but rather opened with a key or lockpick. *Turn to 177.*

324

Conscious of the Colonel's anger, you draw a deep breath before you begin to explain the evidence. If you are wrong, you will be in a great deal of trouble.

• *If you checked Clue Z and Clue FF, turn to 541.*
• *Otherwise, turn to 236.*

325

"There was one other incident that points to Miss Dunlop as the guilty party," you continue, gathering momentum."The thief dropped the eagle into a chair rather than carry it down the ladder. This indicates that the thief was not very strong; this telling weakness points directly at your niece, Colonel." ***Turn to 505.***

326

For a moment, you ponder why the thief dropped the eagle into the chair. It seems an unnecessary risk to you. The thief might have damaged the eagle, or helplessly watched the bird fall to the floor with a crash. Then the answer comes to you. The eagle is not a light bird; it must have been too heavy for the thief to carry down the ladder. Therefore the thief must not have been an exceptionally strong person. *Check Deduction 19.* ***Turn to 106.***

327

Mimicking Watson, you dress with the utmost care, hoping to look as distinguished as the good doctor. Together you go downstairs, joining the other guests in a sitting room for an aperitif. ***Turn to 277.***

328

You begin to search for a way to approach the eagle. It is difficult to see by your candlelight, but you finally conclude that there is only one method to employ. You must go up to the gallery, cross the railing that protects it, and then edge along the decorative molding along the wall until you reach the mantle where the eagle rests. It looks like a very tricky proposition.
• *If you decide to leave,* ***turn to 595.***
• *If you approach the eagle,* ***turn to 197.***

"We're coming into South Riding," Watson explains, tucking away the booklets. "Here, we take the branch line to Gunston, eh?"

Nodding, you follow Watson as you step from your compartment and cross the platform in the clear, warm summer air. At a word from your cousin, a porter points to the local train loading passengers and cargo; you two just have time to climb aboard.

"Not a cloud in the sky," Watson muses, and ever the detective, you immediately spy one on the western horizon. The branch train's seats are hard and seem to be designed at an angle that transmits the full impact of every turn in the track directly into the sorry passenger's rump. You quickly realize that the roadbed could use a attention and begin to count the minutes until you reach your destination. Conversation is impossible above the noise of the growling engine, and the intermediate stops only make the jolting worse. Finally the pair of you reach Gunston. With a gasp of relief Watson staggers from the carriage, with you a step behind. Outside the handsome one-story brick station a liveried servant waits with a well-polished brougham; after a word with Watson, he helps you in. The soft cushions are a delight after the train ride, and the carriage rolls so smoothly that it hardly seems to be moving.

The fresh air and sunshine warm and heal you, and in twenty minutes, the carriage enters the spacious grounds of Eagle Towers, a fine brick mansion placed at the top of a gentle hill. Groves of trees and apple orchards surround the manor. As you dismount from the brougham, the Colonel steps out to greet you warmly and to lead you up to your room. "I'm delighted to see you," he says warmly to Doctor Watson, merely nodding to you. "Wash and change as quickly as you can, gentlemen; then join us for tea in the Library, won't you? The other guests have arrived." A quarter of an hour later, you descend the wide staircase beside your cousin. The library stands just to your left; you can see that it was formerly a part of a grand entrance hall. An arched doorway leads into it from the hall, and as you step through, the Colonel grips your hand and leads you in. 5

The Library is an elegant wood-paneled room two stories high. The shelves that line three sides rise to the ceiling. A gallery circles these shelves at the level of the upper hall, reached by a spiral stair within the library. The fourth wall, which faces the hall's entrance, shelters a grand stone fireplace, with comfortable couches and chairs on either side. The stone mantle rises fifteen feet above the floor, and on this raised shelf the golden Eagle is perched like a gift from the gods. For a moment your eyes are riveted on the treasure — bright gold worked beautifully, and highlighted by many gems.

Then the Colonel proposes to introduce you to the other guests. The first guest you meet, Captain Leaf, is a ruddy-faced, stoutly- built old officer who immediately launches a tale of his adventures in Afghanistan. For a moment, you fear you may not have time to meet any of the other guests today. Happily, you are rescued by a lovely, fair-haired young woman.

"Oh, Uncle Alex," she laughs, scolding your host, "how could you start the poor souls with the Captain? They might never meet the others." To your surprise, Leaf laughs at the joke and drifts off to trap someone else with his tales.

"My niece, Ellen," the Colonel says briefly, clearly worshipping the girl, as she pulls you away.

"And this is my fiance, Robert Harris," she says, presenting you to a lean, tanned, and well-dressed young man. "Robert, these are my uncle's newest guests, Dr. John Watson of London and his cousin, Mr. Hurley." You shake hands with Harris — he has a firm strong grip that seems to match his honest face.

- *If you talk to Harris,* **turn to 154.**
- *Otherwise,* **turn to 590.**

330

Alone in your room with Watson, you discuss what you have learned. "The library is certainly well-protected," Watson comments. "All the doors seem to be solidly secured, and even if a thief entered the library at night, he would be forced to climb to that shelf and pick the locks. I doubt that any one of these gentlemen is up to it."

"Perhaps," you answer thoughtfully, "but how many of the men Mr. Holmes apprehended seemed to you to be criminals when you first met them? Mr. Holmes always says that the most skilled criminals often are ordinary, common- looking men. Would those locks stop a determined burglar?"

"Well, I doubt that you would get the chance to test them," Watson replies.

A gong sounds to summon you to dinner, and you return downstairs. Beach supervises the presentation of a multi-course dinner of fine food and wine. Finally, the women withdraw and leave you and the other men to cigars, port and brandy. As the men chat, a few options present themselves.

• *If you talk with Captain Leaf,* **turn to 127.**
• *If you talk to Robert Harris,* **turn to 432.**
• *If you go outside to look around,* **turn to 308.**

331

You open the dumbwaiter door and see nothing but ropes and the empty chute. Eager to help, Watson tugs at the ropes, but they do not move. Frustrated, you stare at the ropes. ***Pick a number*** *and add your Observation bonus:*

• *If 2-8,* **turn to 289.**
• *If 9-12,* **turn to 257.**

332

Thinking about it, you can understand why the participants in the duel are uneasy; it is uncomfortable to have a gun pointed at you, even if the weapon is loaded with blanks. Miss Mortimer is naturally concerned because her brother and fiance are involved. But why is Grayson the solicitor nervous? He has no part in the duel. Perhaps he has some other personal or business problems unknown to any but himself. *Check Deduction 12.* **Turn to 447.**

333

You look out a window and see that it will rain shortly. Remembering the mud on the ladder, you resolve that now is the time to examine the mud, before the rain washes away any traces.

• *If you examine the mud,* **turn to 158.**
• *Otherwise,* **turn to 196.**

"Where does that door lead, Colonel?" you ask, pointing. "I did not notice it earlier."

"Oh, that," the Colonel replies. "You are very thorough. The door leads into the gun room, but you can see that no one could open it from the other side. It is half-hidden by trophies anyway." You continue to look around the library, wondering whether there are other ways a thief might enter or leave. *Check Clue B*. *Turn to 164*.

"Good grief, Holmes!" cries Dr. Watson, reaching for his cane and bowler. "We must hurry!" *Turn to 350*.

"Here-now, guv, no need for that," Phillips says as you shake the stick at him. "I'll tell you what you want." *Turn to 195*.

"More than a coincidence," surmises Holmes, reaching for his pipe. *Turn to 348*.

"Well, have you identified any potential thieves yet?" Watson asks. He obviously has passed a very enjoyable evening.

"It is not a question of identifying every possible thief," you answer, "but rather one of making it impossible for anyone to take the eagle."

"You cannot do anything more tonight, can you?" Watson asks. "It is late, cousin. Are you planning to wait until everyone has gone to bed and then check the security of the library?" He laughs at the very idea, obviously intending it to be a joke. But you stop to consider the matter. Are the library's defenses as secure as the Colonel believes?

- *If you go to bed, turn to 187.*
- *If you look over the library, turn to 169.*

339

You stretch a little, then pick up your book again. Before you resume reading, Beach comes in with a light lunch. You thank him and enjoy a cucumber sandwich. You almost wish that you had gone to the duel — it would have been a sight worth seeing, and no one has threatened the eagle. Suddenly, you hear the front door thrown open, and the gasping voice of Ellen Dunlop calling for the servants. You run to the hall and find her leaning against the wall.

"Oh, good, you are still here," she gasps. "There was a terrible accident at the duel, sir. Somehow, Mr. Snead's gun was loaded, and John Mortimer was wounded in the neck. Would you go back there with the servants and see if you can help? They will take a cot and blankets. I shall prepare a bedroom." Naturally, you cannot refuse such a request, especially from such a lovely young lady. You leave the house with the servants, although they do not seem to need your help. At the site of the duel, they set the cot down beside the injured man. ***Turn to 478.***

340

"Come, come, man, you accused my niece," the Colonel growls, "You must have some proof for that absurd charge."

You desperately search for the proper explanation.
• *If you checked Clue EE, **turn to 100**.*
• *Otherwise, **turn to 113**.*

341

Nearly defeated by the hard ground and dense underbrush, you are almost ready to give up when a broken twig on a tree catches your eye. You approach the tree and find another broken branch a few yards away; caught in the branch are two or three threads. Calling to the others to join you, you follow the "trail," managing to keep your way by spotting broken branches and occasional partial footprints on the ground. You come to a cleared path, too hard-packed for any footprints to show, but in a hollow tree you see an odd shape and find a rifle! You recognize it as one of Colonel Dunlop's guns, and a quick examination proves that it has been fired recently. You start down the path, hoping to discover some clue that might identify the marksman. *Check Clue W. **Pick a number** and add your Observation bonus:*

- *If 2-8, **turn to 190**.*
- *If 9-12, **turn to 253**.*

342

You display a skill at rock-throwing that you didn't know you had. In the midst of tossing a barrage of stones that must have frightened every animal for miles around, you hit the largest pan with your first toss and the second biggest with two tries. Dr. Cunningham is the only other contestant to hit the third pan. Now the competition seems more serious. You draw a deep breath before throwing at the smallest pan, the tension increasing after the doctor hits the target with his first shot. "You must hit the pan with your first throw to remain in the competition, Mister Hurley," Miss Dunlop announces.

After a quiet, tense moment of concentration, you are pleased to make the pan clang. You take your second throw first, and the small pan chimes like a church bell, spinning around and around on its rope. The doctor looks confident as he steps up and throws, but even as he lets loose with the stone, the rope begins to spin back in the opposite direction. The movement obviously distracts him, and his stone misses by a hair.

"Oh, you must throw again, doctor," Miss Dunlop says, "that wasn't fair!"

Before you have a chance to agree, the doctor shakes his head. "No, no," he laughs, "I just missed, no blame to the rope. This young man is the winner." He quickly shakes your hand and raises it above your head. The others pat you on your back and join in congratulating you, while you thank the doctor for his courtesy and sportsmanship. Then Miss Dunlop leads the whole group across the stream and into the woods, where you follow a shady path under the trees. ***Turn to 431.***

You return to your room and go to bed, pleased that you have taken some extra action to protect the eagle. When your sleep is deepest, a loud crash brings you to your feet before your eyes are fully open. "My word, the trap!" Watson cries. You and Watson run toward the library, pulling on dressing gowns as you stumble down the stairs.

The entire household is clustered around the library entrance in a matter of moments. The Colonel asks everyone but you to remain in the hall; then he opens the door and lights a lamp. A thorough examination reveals that no one is in the room and that all the doors are secure, although a pile of objects you used for the trap lie in plain sight by the fireplace. You explain your failed trap to the enraged Colonel; unhappily, the unanimous opinion of the group is that you are an utter fool. *(Reduce your Communication bonus by one for the remainder of the adventure.)*

"But who set off the trap?" Watson asks, amid the round of harsh words and condemnations. Suddenly, a small gray form runs out of a corner and leaps into Miss Dunlop's arms.

"Bootsie," she murmurs softly, stroking the cat. "So you are the big, bad burglar."

Knowing that nothing you say could possibly help, you slink back to bed without a word of explanation. Fortunately, when you go down to breakfast, your fellow guests seem to have readmitted you into their select group. (You had wondered if anyone would talk to you again.) ***Turn to 599.***

344

The Colonel leads you back upstairs to your bedroom, pointing out who has the other rooms as he passes them. Then he shows you a door that must lead into the library gallery. "There is another way to get into the library," he explains, "but I locked it from the other side, and bolted it at the top and the bottom of the door. Only a professional burglar could force it open." *Check Clue E.* **Turn to 330.**

345

It is late afternoon when you and the other guests return to the house. With only a quick cup of tea to tide one over, everyone goes to his rooms to wash and change for dinner. The Colonel has warned you that dinner will be served a little early.

Everything is laid out for you and Watson in your room. As you prepare for dinner, you chat a little about the day's contests. ***Pick a number*** *and add your Observation bonus:*
• *If 2-6,* **turn to 327.**
• *If 7-12,* **turn to 535.**

346

"I have solid physical proof of her guilt," you say quietly. "There was mud on the library ladder, mud from the patch on the path near the duelling ground. Only one person ran through that mud: Miss Ellen Dunlop."
• *If you checked Clue FF,* **turn to 570.**
• *Otherwise,* **turn to 201.**

Wondering if it will do you any good, you begin to read through the history of the Yorkshire Light Artillery. Quickly, you realize that the battery is not a permanent army unit, but rather is a reserve unit activated when expansion of the army is necessary. In spite of this status, however, it enjoyed a long and gallant history, serving with Wellington in the Peninsula and at Waterloo; the Yorkshire Lights were activated again for the Crimean War and later saw action in Africa in the 1870's. Your host, Colonel Dunlop, was its last commander. So succesful was he, that he was promoted and given command of several batteries in Afghanistan.

The Eagle, called "The Honour of The Yorkshire Lights" in the pamphlet, was made from gold and jewels looted from the French at the Battle of Vittoria in 1813. According to the account, the "Honour" was carved from oak, then covered in gold, and finally decorated with diamonds, rubies and pearls. It is kept in a bank vault in York, except for the week of the annual reunion. As you read through the battle accounts that dot the history, you come across one interesting event that is annually staged at the reunion. It seems that in 1815, only a few days before the Battle of Waterloo, two junior officers named Snead and Mortimer exchanged shots in a duel. A widower, Snead planned to marry Mortimer's sister and was insulted when Mortimer blocked the ceremony. In the duel, Mortimer fired quickly and missed. Snead, known to be a dead shot, deliberately fired over Mortimer's head. Though the post-duel courtesies revealed that a mutual dislike remained, the Battle of Waterloo brought out the men's true mettle.

Amid the horrors of that day, each man saved the other's life more than once, although both men suffered mortal wounds before the sun had set on Wellington's victory. Their shared gallantry assumed a place in the regiment's history equal to that of winning the eagle. The duel is "refought" every year at Colonel Dunlop's reunion. Lost in the pamphlet's account of the Siege of Sevastopol in 1856, you feel the train begin to slow. Looking up, you see Watson stowing his own book in his coat pocket and checking his other luggage. *Check Clue A.* **Turn to 329.**

348

"If he is innocent, then who is the guilty party?" asks Dr.Watson, perplexed. ***Turn to 335.***

349

You find Colonel Dunlop seated in the library and explain that you have been unable to uncover more evidence regarding the shooting.
• *If you checked Clue X,* ***turn to 451.***
• *Otherwise,* ***turn to 124.***

350

"I should be more careful with that rapier," suggests Holmes, puffing on his pipe. ***Turn to 337.***

351

You study the locks and consider what you have seen, calling up all that you have learned about lockpicking. After a minute or two of careful consideration, you feel certain of your interpretation of the facts. Someone used the key to open the padlocks! There are no marks or scratches of the type that even the best lockpick would leave. *Check Clue GG.* ***Turn to 177.***

352

Though the dresser and wardrobe yield nothing of interest, you are more fortunate when you search the desk. In the top drawer you find a large ring of keys. They look as though they were put away, not hidden, in the desk. You look at them for a moment, then understand. Miss Dunlop helps her uncle run the house — obviously she would need to have a set of keys to the place. Looking over the keys, you find one that seems to fit the padlock. Testing it, you find that it fits the lock. *Check Clue EE.* ***Turn to 153.***

353

Although concerned that the Colonel is displeased with you, you are pleased that he orders Grayson to leave. At least the criminal will not be able to repeat his attempt.

It is more difficult to face Holmes in the morning and to admit that you failed due to your own lack of discretion. You return to London and Baker Street with Holmes and Watson, and several weeks pass before you learn the motive for the shooting. *Turn to 462.*

354

"I have no idea why Grayson shot Mortimer," you unhappily admit, shrugging your shoulders. "I suppose his motive will emerge if he is brought to trial."

"I doubt that charges will be brought," Holmes comments, cutting you off sharply. "The scandal would be much too harmful. However, I know why the shooting occurred."

You lean closer to hear, and Watson looks at you as if to say: 'How does he do it?'

"I read a very strange old will, this afternoon, at the local courthouse," continues Mr. Holmes. "Under its terms, a large sum of money is to be paid to Mr. Snead and Miss Mortimer when they wed. Grayson is the sole trustee; I know something of his business affairs. He has undoubtedly tied that money up in his enterprises, so that delivering it to the happy couple — as he was required to do — would ruin him. I dislike all such wills in principle," Holmes adds. "They are an invitation to dishonesty." He then begins to answer Watson's questions regarding his quick solution of the jewel thefts. Although you try to listen, you find your thoughts drifting away, as you wonder what challenges and dangers your next investigation will bring. The End

355

Having completed your examination of the eagle, you look for a way down. You see that there is a soft chair to one side of the mantle and manage to drop onto it, then stepping safely to the floor. You are relieved to complete the 'expedition' in one piece. *Turn to 595.*

356

Pleased with yourself, you reach in among the ropes and remove the piece of wire that held them together. Then you work the ropes and lower the tray back into sight. Sitting majestically upon it is the golden bird!

"I say!" cries the Colonel, reaching for the treasured standard. *Turn to 589.*

357

You test the key from Snead's chest in the library padlock. At first try it will not turn in the lock, but you twist it a little and suddenly the lock pops open in your hand. Snead could have unfastened the eagle from its bonds! But did he? *Check Deduction 24. Turn to 107.*

358

While the padlocks are heavy and formidable, you recall that this particular make of lock is easily opened by a lock-pick. If a thief were to reach the mantle, it might not take him much time to free the eagle. *Turn to 355.*

359

As the Colonel rambles on, you notice a door in the inner wall, an entrance almost hidden by two huge battle flags. "Where does that little door lead?" you ask the Colonel, interrupting his lecture.

"Oh, that," he says in an offhand way. "You need not worry about that. It leads into the library, but it is locked from the other side and bolted top and bottom. A thief might be able to use it to escape from the library, but he would have to be a very skillful villain to enter the library by this route."

"Thank you," you answer, glancing around for any other significant exits. The Colonel launches into the story of the standards, which almost hide the small portal. *Check Clue B. Turn to 487.*

Colonel Dunlop looks at the prisoner, then laughs. "You again, Badger," he says, clearly amused rather than upset. "Can you not learn to leave my birds alone?"

"What are you going to do with him?" Mortimer asks in menacing anticipation. "I cannot do anything tonight," Dunlop answers. "Phillips," he continues, addressing the prisoner, "Come to my study Tuesday morning at ten. I will pass my judgment then."

As Badger Phillips leaves, you notice Dr. Watson going upstairs and follow him quickly. *Turn to 338.*

Perhaps the intruder left behind a piece of evidence that might identify him. The bright moonlight will help in your examination. *Pick a number and add your Observation bonus: (Add 3 if you have the magnifying glass.)*
• *If 2-7, turn to 240.*
• *If 8-12, turn to 395.*

"Why would anyone care whether Snead marries Susan Mortimer?" the Colonel demands, barely able to keep his voice down. "I can conceive of no reason for such obstructive behavior."
• *If you have not checked Decision 17 and wish to talk to Captain Leaf, turn to 532.*
• *If you have not checked Decision 16 and wish to talk to Dr. Cunningham, turn to 204.*
• *If you have completed the interviews, turn to 349.*

You notice that one end of the table has been cleared by the servants. Watson and Cunningham stand together there, laying out bandages and surgical instruments, just as if they might have to treat a gunshot wound! *Turn to 320.*

364

As Jackson concludes his comment, you understand Grayson's motive. "Grayson could thus benefit from shooting Mortimer," you say, "or at least delay the inevitable financial disaster." As the others (except Leaf) look at you in surprise, you explain: "Grayson is the trustee of an estate that will belong to Mr. Snead and Miss Mortimer when they wed." You pause as a gasp arises from the group. "If Grayson had used that money to finance his investments, withdrawing it to give to the couple would ruin him. Thus, he hoped to prevent the marriage by wounding Lieutenant Mortimer in a manner that could cast the shadow of guilt upon Snead."

As you pause, the others eagerly discuss what you have said. Then Captain Leaf tells them more about of the will. All of the guests seem to agree that your conclusions, however sad, are probably correct. *Turn to 165.*

365

As you try to open the padlock, you hear a loud click, and it falls open in your hand. You can enter the library now and realize that any other skilled intruder could probably do the same. *Check Deduction 8.*

• *If you go into the library, turn to 409.*
• *Otherwise, turn to 393.*

366

"Someone tried to make it appear that Snead shot Mortimer," you note. Holmes rolls his eyes at the simplicity of your deduction. "The marksman must have been trying to settle some grudge against Snead."

"And is Mr. Snead such an unpleasant man?" Holmes asks, almost sneering. "What do you mean, Holmes?" Watson asks. "Why should Snead be an unpleasant fellow?"

"It would take a very nasty fellow indeed to provoke such a plot," Holmes answers, "especially among a group of people who had known him for only a few weeks. Perhaps our friend would like to try again?" Again those piercing grey eyes are turned on you.

- *If you blame it on hatred for Mortimer, **turn to 559**.*
- *If you call if an attempt to stop the wedding, **turn to 156**.*

367

Moving with considerable stealth, you cautiously approach the intruder. To your surprise, he is handling the pair of old duelling pistols which the Colonel showed you the afternoon before. The intruder turns slightly, and you estimate his size. From his height, you realize that it must be Snead, Grayson, Foxx or Miss Mortimer, if indeed this intruder is one of the weekend guests.

If you can get a step or two closer, you should be able to tackle the intruder, call for Watson, and solve this small mystery. *Check Clues F and G. **Turn to 133**.*

"Yes, the jewel thefts," you add to Miss Dunlop's remark, "I suppose they concern everyone at the moment. It suggests rare nerve for a thief to strike twice in a week."

Harris laughs with you. "Your cufflinks should be safe," he comments snidely. "I should think that any thief at Eagle's Towers would certainly snatch the eagle and ignore any other trifles. But you know, I almost fear that no one will have me as a guest in the future."

"Oh, why is that?" you ask with an innocent air about you.

"Well," he smiles, "I happened to be a guest at both houses that were victims of the villain. If there are any more thefts in my presence, I'm likely to pass my next holiday at Scotland Yard!"

"Oh, don't say such a thing," Ellen laughs, playfully hitting her fiance on the arm. "Come, Robert; find me some tea and muffins," she insists, dragging him away. *Turn to 590.*

You decide that you will not find any more useful information upstairs, and that searching there would be a waste of time. *Turn to 579.*

"What do you ship?" you ask Snead.

"Oh, various items," he answers evasively. "Shipping is the art of getting things from where they are to where they are needed. In a rough country like Canada, you must use every means at your disposal. I really cannot say much more," he adds obliquely. "I would not want my plans to become public knowledge."

You glance at Watson, who has joined you, and see the same question in his eyes: could the mysterious Mr. Snead's "shipping business" be merely a euphemism for smuggling? Regardless, it would be useless to inquire further at this time. *Turn to 385.*

"I am not at all certain why Grayson assaulted you, Lieutenant Mortimer," you say slowly. "I know that he needs money desperately, but I have no idea how he could help himself by shooting you."

As the others regard your comment, Captain Leaf's eyes open wide, and he says sharply: "But I know."

"What do you know, Eric?" Colonel Dunlop asks.

"I know why Grayson shot at Mortimer," Leaf answers. "It is because of old Colonel Murphy's will. The Colonel was very impressed by the circumstances of the original Snead-Mortimer duel, and the reason they fought. As he died without heirs, he stipulated that his estate be held in trust until a Snead and Mortimer married, the money then go to the newlyweds. Grayson is currently the trustee. Perhaps he invested the money in some failing enterprise and faces personal ruin if he were forced to pay it out." *Turn to 165.*

372

The greyish-colored mud means nothing to you. It will be no help unless you are fortunate enough to find the shoe that left the mud on the ladder. *Turn to 428.*

373

Having completed your talk, you and Captain Leaf return to watch the finish of the billiard match. *Turn to 131.*

374

As you think over the story, you feel sure that Grayson arranged to be invited to Eagle Towers for the weekend. You wonder if he had any motive beyond enjoying a luxurious weekend. *Check Deduction 3. Turn to 315.*

375

At your earlier request, the Colonel has already given you a key to the padlocks on the library gates, so that you are not forced to pick the locks to get in. You and Watson go down to the library and consider the best method to protect it from unwanted entry. *Pick a number and add your Artifice bonus:*
• *If 2-7, turn to 312.*
• *If 8-12, turn to 397.*

You visit the downstairs bedroom where Mortimer is resting, and talk for a while with him, his sister and Snead. Gradually you bring the talk around to a very important question: "Would anyone benefit by preventing the marriage?" The trio is mystified at the very idea, even after you mention Grayson. Thanking them, you ask them not to speak of your conversation and leave. You wonder whom to seek out next.

- *If you have not checked Decision 15 and wish to talk to Colonel Dunlop, turn to 440.*
- *If you have not checked Decision 16 and wish to talk to Dr. Cunningham, turn to 204.*
- *If you have not checked Decision 17 and wish to talk to Captain Leaf, turn to 532.*

You find that throwing a rock accurately is a more challenging task than you had expected and cannot hit the largest pan in the alloted three attempts. When the others reject your claim that the last rock's contact with the smallest pan was intentional, you are forced to sit on a log and watch. Surprisingly, old Dr. Cunningham wins easily; none of the younger men or women hits the second smallest pan. *Turn to 431.*

"You know, cousin," Watson finally says, "I cannot name a prime suspect who might carry out the theft. You must ensure that no one can get at the eagle and not just guard against a particular individual."

"What should I do that I have not done?" you ask.

"I have one idea," he says, a little timidly. "Perhaps you could arrange some kind of alarm in the library, one that would catch an intruder."

- *If you set an alarm, turn to 375.*
- *Otherwise, turn to 585.*

379

You come to the point where you might have intercepted Grayson and find some signs on the trail that he is gone. Is it worth the effort to continue running after a solicitor out for a stroll? Chagrined, you return to the house and pick up your book again. The dining room clock strikes noon. *Turn to 160.*

380

The empty library is so quiet that you imagine hearing the sound of your candle burning. Then, from across the room, you hear a small scraping noise between a couch and the bookcase. It startles you for a moment; then you smile, certain that it is only a mouse. *Turn to 272.*

381

As noon draws near, you find yourself alone, glancing at the others. Foxx has begun the task of loading the guns, while the elder Mortimers are talking earnestly to their daughter.
• *If you watch Foxx load the guns,* **turn to 192.**
• *If you try to overhear the Mortimers,* **turn to 125.**
• *Otherwise,* **turn to 408.**

"I believe that Mr. Grayson stole the Eagle," you say. "I have kept an eye on him since our arrival, for I know that he needs capital badly."

"The desire for capital does not make a man a thief," Holmes says coldly. "As it happens, I can vouch for Mr. Grayson myself. He rode from town with me, and I saw him paying for telegrams in Gunston when I went to the post office to send one at one o'clock. He could not have committed the theft and reached town in the interval of time available." *Turn to 540.*

"Where are the other doors to the dumbwaiter?" you ask Dunlop. "Do you use it regularly?"

"We do not use it at all," the Colonel answers, shaking his head in exasperation. "This is the only remaining entrance - the others are walled up. Even if they were open, the thing does not work properly. It will not go down at all, and does not rise high enough to reach the old second floor exit."

• *If you look inside the dumbwaiter,* **turn to 476.**
• *Otherwise,* **turn to 224.**

As you look around the library, you notice that there is a small door, just to the right of the fireplace. Aside from its lock, shining bolts secure it at the top and bottom of its frame.

• *If you checked Clue B,* **turn to 434.**
• *Otherwise,* **turn to 216.**

You continue to talk politely with Snead about upcoming events at the Towers and wonder how he managed to became engaged to Miss Mortimer so quickly. She seems to come from the sort of stuffy, conservative family that would object to her marrying a man she had known for only a few months.

• *If you ask him about his romance,* **turn to 438.**
• *Otherwise,* **turn to 436.**

386

You recount the story of the prowler of the first night and ask the Colonel if you might examine the pistols. He agrees, and you carefully lift them from their case. The pistols are a matched pair, masterpieces of the gunmaker's art. They have heavy mahogany butts and engraved steel barrels, trimmed in silver. Although they are seventy-five years old, they seem to be in perfect condition. ***Pick a number** and add your Observation bonus: (Add 3 if you have a magnifying glass.)*

• *If 2-9,* **turn to 545.**

• *If 10-12,* **turn to 117.**

387

You realize that if you leave the door unlocked, either the Colonel or Beach will certainly notice it and make some comment in the morning. You wonder whether you should try to lock it again, although you are not certain that you can, without the key.

• *If you try to lock it,* **turn to 509.**

• *Otherwise,* **turn to 223.**

388

Captain Leaf pauses for a moment to sip his port, and you manage to speak before he can swallow. "It is very kind of you to talk with me, Captain," you begin, smiling. "I feel like an outsider here. All the rest of you seem to have some connection to each other, and with the affairs of the weekend, and I have nothing to do with any of it. My cousin was planning to bring another friend with him and only invited me at the last minute."

"Oh, you must not feel that way," Leaf says hurriedly, "not at all, young man. Why, young Harris and old Grayson could be called outsiders as well. Harris is only here to visit his fiance, and Grayson happened to be at Jackson's when the Colonel stopped there on his way back from London."

"You are very kind," you suggest to Leaf.

"I assure you sir, you are very welcome," the Captain says heartily. "Just join in the various outings we have scheduled, do your best, and by the time you leave Monday morning we shall consider you a colleague of twenty years standing. Upon my word, sir, I've seen things happen that way time and again. You will see; I assure you."

• *If you ask him about the eagle, **turn to 600**.*
• *If you ask about the outings, **turn to 246**.*

389

Carefully you edge along the molding towards the eagle. Your respect for the Colonel's security arrangements increases when your right foot slips from the molding, and you fall heavily. Fortunately, a couch breaks your fall and muffles the noise. Relieved to survive the accident without injury or disturbance, you rise, if somewhat slowly, and head for the library door. ***Turn to 595.***

390

After a long period of quiet, you hear a noise from the gun room. After a moment's consideration, you go in to check the source of the noise. No one is there, and you find no evidence of a recent intruder. As you study the scene, Colonel Dunlop and Watson enter the room. "We came for the duelling pistols," the Colonel explains, examining you suspiciously. "What are you doing here?"

"I thought I heard a noise," you explain. "I appear to have been mistaken." Acting in a ceremonious fashion, the Colonel picks up the case of pistols and passes them to the doctor, who carefully sets it on a table and opens it. You recall that Watson too was once a military man.

• *If you checked Clue F, **turn to 552**.*
• *Otherwise, **turn to 426**.*

391

With Watson's help, you manage to rig the thread and shove it under the hall door. Then you walk upstairs and take it into your room.

You sleep well that night, for the bell does not disturb your slumber. When you go down to breakfast in the morning, you carefully remove any evidence of the trap. *Turn to 599.*

392

"Lieutenant Jackson and Captain Leaf worked together to steal the eagle," you announce somewhat uncertainly. "They were together in the drawing room, next to the library. If they were not the thieves, they should have heard something."

Holmes shakes his head in amazement. "I am sorry, Watson," he says to the Doctor. "You do not deserve the scorn which I have heaped upon some of your theories, if your cousin can invent charges of this magnitude of imbecility. The very idea that two officers, scarcely acquainted before this weekend, should conspire on the spur of the moment to steal the eagle is folly worthy of Gregson or Lestrade on their worst day. Surely you have been taught better than that!" *Turn to 540.*

393

Outside the library, you stop to consider what further actions to take tonight. Are there other approaches to the library that you might examine?
• *If you checked Clue B, **turn to 450.***
• *Otherwise, **turn to 410.***

Holmes sees you and Watson as soon as you see him (of course) and greets you warmly. "You are early, my friends," he says chuckling. "Colonel Dunlop must not be feeding you properly. Come; the innkeeper has a private room ready for us and can begin serving at any time." Then Holmes' voice changes as he adds: "And you can tell me what has happened." The innkeeper leads the three of you to a small room, where spotless linen covers a round table. A moment later the little round fellow returns with your soup, and as he vanishes, Holmes says quietly: "Now, tell me: what has happened? Did someone steal that eagle? I no longer worried about it when I captured the culprits in the other thefts. Those two crimes were not connected, by the way, as you may have reasoned from newspaper accounts."

"No, the eagle is not gone, Holmes," Watson says grimly, perhaps defending your prowess as a detective. "But the re-creation of the duel ended in bloodshed, due to a gunman hidden in the woods."

Holmes looks astonished for a moment, then says grimly: "Tell me about it." You carefully explain everything that happened at Eagle Towers, pausing only when the servants come and go with the succeeding courses of your dinner.
- *If you checked Clue X,* ***turn to 198.***
- *Otherwise,* ***turn to 247.***

You examine the window very carefully and smile in satisfaction. You discover several brown hairs caught in a crack in the window frame. The short hairs must belong to a man. Only three men you have met this weekend have hair that color — Badger Phillips, Snead and Grayson. *Check Clue H.* ***Turn to 152.***

396

You visit the town hall and find the chief clerk. The small, merry chap allows you to look through the local records, thanks to Holmes' note of introduction, but he can offer you no other guidance. *Pick a number and add your Scholarship bonus:*
• *If 2-7,* ***turn to 500.***
• *If 8-12,* ***turn to 453.***

397

You recognize the possibility that someone might get around an alarm, but you devise a method to indicate if anyone has tampered with either the gun room or hall door. If you melt some wax so that it connects the door and doorframe, you will be able to tell if anyone has opened the door.
• *If you mark the door with wax,* ***turn to 402.***
• *Otherwise,* ***turn to 312.***

398

"She also has keys to open the padlocks," you continue.

"My niece has keys to every lock in the house," the Colonel admits.

"And," you add, "the thief knew the house well. Obviously your niece would know everything about the house."
• *If you checked Deduction 19,* ***turn to 212.***
• *Otherwise,* ***turn to 505.***

399

You look over the door but find it is locked; the inside bolts are still fastened. Whatever her intentions, Miss Mortimer did not do anything to the door. You and Watson quickly join the other guests in the sitting room for an apertif. ***Turn to 277.***

400

"I agree," you admit. "His behaviour has been exactly what you would expect of a man in his position. I hope he is innocent — it would hurt a very sweet young lady if he proved to be a cad." ***Turn to 193.***

401

Miss Dunlop seems to consider the question for a long moment. "I left the bedroom as soon as I saw that Dr. Cunningham had everything under control and did not require my help. I needed to go upstairs and change, as my shoes and clothes were muddy. But I hesitated a moment as I left John's room, for I saw Robert Snead outside the library, just standing there. Then he went upstairs, and I followed a minute later." *Check Clue BB*. *Pick a number* and add your Intuition bonus:
• *If 2-7, turn to 483.*
• *If 8-12, turn to 419.*

402

You use candle wax to form a seal across the bottom of the doors, carefully scraping the excess from the floor. The wax is visible, but not too obvious to the eye. *Check Decision 20. Turn to 312.*

403

You continue talking with Dr. Watson and Captain Leaf until the Colonel's coach returns. Beach gracefully opens the door and Holmes' tall, lean figure strides in. As always he appears eager for the chase. You and Watson join Holmes and the Colonel in the Colonel's study, where he outlines the case to the detective. You then tell Holmes everything that you have been able to learn. Holmes listens carefully, then goes outside to investigate, guided by Redruth the Groundskeeper. Holmes spends almost two hours outside investigating, and his clothes show signs of having gone through heavy grass and brush when he returns. Again you join him, the Colonel, and Dr. Watson in the study. "Well, Mr. Holmes," the Colonel begins, "who is the guilty party?"

"I think you should ask my associate first," Holmes answers primly, indicating you. "It is his case, after all. I know who committed the various acts which so disturbed the peace at Eagle Towers, but he should receive the credit if he has indeed solved the case." Reluctantly the Colonel agrees.
• *If you checked Decision 23, turn to 142.*
• *Otherwise, turn to 254.*

404

You begin to hunt along the edge of the woods, trying to find some evidence that might help you identify the gunman or locate the direction in which he fled. The ground is rough and wild; you find the task difficult. *Pick a number and add your Observation bonus: (Add 3 if you checked Clue T.)*
• If 2-9, *turn to 539.*
• If 10-12, *turn to 217.*

405

You decide that setting a trap would do more harm than good. With Watson, you quietly return to your bedroom. *Turn to 585.*

406

With a start, you notice that one of the rifles is missing from the rack by the window and point out its absence to the Colonel. "That's hardly surprising, young man" says your host. "One of the men must have taken it to shoot at some birds. It will be back before nightfall, I am sure." *Check Clue P. Turn to 417.*

407

Wondering how secure it is, you try to pick the lock to the door to the library. For a moment, you study the lock and try to remember everything you know about the art of lockpicking. *Pick a number and add your Artifice bonus: (Add 4 if you have the skeleton keys):*
• If 2-9, *turn to 189.*
• If 10-12, *turn to 265.*

408

With no one to talk to, you relax and look around, trying to note any odd behavior on the part of your fellow guests. Holmes insists that constant practice will increase any man's skill at the art of observation. *Pick a number and add your Observation bonus:*
• If 2-4, *turn to 555.*
• If 5-8, *turn to 414.*
• If 9-12, *turn to 363.*

409

Carefully you unthread the chain from the bars and lay it on the drawing room carpet. Sliding the gates apart, you slip between them.

The library is a strange place in the dark, lit only by the moon, and starlight that filters in from neighboring rooms. Your candle provides only enough light to guide your footsteps safely. At your sign, Watson waits outside. A few steps into the library you stop and listen. *Pick a number and add your Observation bonus:*

- *If 2-5, turn to 272.*
- *If 6-8, turn to 463.*
- *If 9-12, turn to 380.*

410

You have considered every route by which someone might enter the library and know as much about protecting the eagle as anyone does. Quietly, you tell Watson that you are ready to return to your bedroom and get a little sleep. Even in the dark, you can discern the doctor's expression of relief. *Turn to 187.*

411

You begin to examine the lock and bolts of this door very carefully, certain that there must be a clue that will help your investigation. *Pick a number and add your Observation bonus: (Add 2 if you have the magnifying glass.)*

- *If 2-7, turn to 105.*
- *If 8-12, turn to 203.*

412

You bend down by the door into the upstairs hall. The wax you placed there remains intact. Thus, no one has used this door since last night. *Turn to 490.*

413

Wandering towards the house, you are surprised to hear one of the clocks chiming ten o'clock. You walk inside and find a triumphant Watson pocketing his winnings from the billiards match. Weary from the day's events, you and the victor climb the stairs to your room. *Turn to 145.*

Looking around, you see Colonel Dunlop, Captain Leaf, and Dr. Cunningham standing close together looking at something in their hands. Their position puzzles you for a moment; then you realize that they must be synchronizing their watches. *Turn to 320.*

You cannot refuse the Colonel's invitation to watch the re-creation of the duel. Everyone (except Grayson and Harris) leaves in a group at about eleven o'clock in the morning. It is a fine, bright morning with only a few high cirrus clouds in the blue sky. The group walks through the quiet woods to a clearing half a mile from the house. There, servants bring out a long table, and a light repast of wine, tea, sandwiches and cakes, which they set up along the edge of the clearing. As everyone begins eating, Jackson and Colonel Dunlop formally pace off the ground and mark the spots where the duellists will stand. Foxx, Cunningham, Watson and Mortimers' parents stand near the center of the table. Prominent on the table is the case containing the duelling pistols. You notice that neither Mortimer nor Snead eats anything, although both sample the wine. *Pick a number and add your Intuition bonus:*

• *If 2-7, turn to 256.*
• *If 8-12, turn to 544.*

416

The duellists wait, standing in their places, their sides pointing toward the opponent (to reduce the target), gun arms by their sides. You wonder what to watch during the duel.
• *If you watch Snead closely,* **turn to 507.**
• *If you watch Mortimer closely,* **turn to 529.**
• *If you watch the entire scene,* **turn to 457.**

417

Watson and the Colonel prepare to leave the gun room. "Are you certain that you will not come to the duel with us?" the Colonel asks. "I should be very pleased if you would join us."

"Yes, cousin, you really must come," Watson insists. "It is the highlight of the weekend, you know."
• *If you attend the duel, erase your check on Decision 26 and* **turn to 415.**
• *Otherwise,* **turn to 239.**

418

"At your urging, I shall keep an eye on Phillips," you assure Watson. "I too saw him lurking about tonight. Still, it is highly unlikely that he would extend his poaching from partridge to eagles, eh?" ***Turn to 433.***

419

You feel that Miss Dunlop is not telling you the whole truth, but you do not dare confront her. Either she saw Snead do something that thoroughly compromised his innocence, or else she knows he is innocent but wishes to protect someone else. Why? ***Turn to 483.***

420

You go upstairs by yourself and slowly walk down the hall. Outside Snead's room, you decide exactly what to do. 'Shall I search the rooms of all three suspects?' you wonder.
• *If you search Snead's room,* **turn to 230.**
• *Otherwise,* **turn to 512.**

421

"Stealing the eagle was a very foolish thing to do!" the Colonel snaps."Now take me to its hiding place at once!" Subdued, Ellen Dunlop leads you and the Colonel into the library. There, she unfastens some wire from the dumbwaiter's ropes, lowers it, and presents the gleaming eagle to her astonished uncle. With your help, he carries to and locks it in his safe.

Then the Colonel returns to the others, with you and his guilty niece in tow. Clearing his throat, he says: "I am pleased to announce that the eagle has been recovered!" Applause breaks out. After extending his thanks to you, the Colonel pours wine for all. You alone seem to notice that he did not name the thief, nor her motivation. ***Turn to 579***.

422

You join the billiards game, teamed with Watson against the two older men. While you and Captain Leaf do not disgrace yourselves, it is obvious that both doctors are masters of the cue. After the first match ends, you join Captain Leaf in urging the two doctors to compete against each other as you and the Captain watch.

The two doctors are excellent players and strategists, each making successful shots and positioning the balls so that his opponent has little chance to score. You and Leaf stand near a door that leads to the sitting room where the whist game is being played. Between hands, you hear sharp comments passing between Snead and Lieutenant Mortimer. To your surprise, Leaf appears pleased at these outbursts of anger.

• *If you have not checked Clue D and you wish to talk to Leaf,* **turn to 510.**
• *Otherwise,* **turn to 131.**

423

You feel certain that Foxx did nothing untoward to the guns, although he might have slipped a ball into one gun without your seeing it. But you can think of no reason why he would do such a thing. ***Turn to 320.***

424

"I suspect Grayson because I do not understand why he is here," you explain to Watson. "With an object as valuable as the eagle to be protected, I must be very suspicious. Even a solicitor might be tempted by an object so valuable."

"So might a doctor," Watson answers, laughing. "Perhaps you should watch me as well."
• *If you checked Clue K,* **turn to 564.**
• *Otherwise,* **turn to 261.**

425

You continue to follow Grayson. To your surprise, you come to a long, narrow millpond that seems to block your way. The water shimmers in the sunlight. The only boat in sight rests on the grassy shore just ahead, and the solicitor takes it. Your pursuit seems to have come to a dead end. *Pick a number and add your Scholarship bonus:*

- *If 2-9, turn to 252.*
- *If 10-12, turn to 102.*

426

Watson takes each gun from the case and checks to see that they are clean and empty. Shielding them from the glare of the sun, he cocks each one and snaps the trigger, to be certain that flints flash brightly. Satisfied, he then returns them to the case and tucks it under one arm. *Pick a number* and add your *Observation bonus:*

- *If 2-7, turn to 417.*
- *If 8-12, turn to 406.*

427

You have thought this over carefully and explain the matter to Mr. Holmes and Dr. Watson at some length. "By shooting Mortimer, an act that would surely be blamed on Snead, Grayson reasoned that he could prevent the wedding between Miss Mortimer and Mr. Snead. Likely Grayson was caught in a business situation wherein the loss of the money he controlled as trustee would ruin him." Having summarized your conclusions, you sit back to hear what the great detective has to say. Will he be pleased?

Holmes briefly congratulates you upon your success; then he begins to explain to you and Watson how he solved the jewel thefts so quickly. In spite of the topic, you find your interest drifting — already you wonder who and what your next case will involve. The End

428

Satisfied that you have learned everything that you can from the ladder, you set it back against the mantle and climb up to look where the eagle had rested. You carefully examine the chains that had held the eagle in place. The big padlocks that held them lie opened on the mantle. *Pick a number and add your Observation bonus:*

• *If 2-5, turn to 167.*
• *If 6-8, turn to 323.*
• *If 9-12, turn to 351.*

429

"You know, Cousin John," you say softly, "I somehow doubt that one thief committed both crimes. The first crime appears to be an 'inside job,' as they say, while the second is more likely the work of an opportunistic burglar."

"That may be," Watson says, chuckling, "but whether there was one thief or two — or ten! — we shall have a difficult time explaining matters to Holmes if the jeweled eagle is stolen while we are there." *Check Deduction 1. Turn to 468.*

"I know one man who hated Mortimer," you reply. "Badger Phillips, the poacher, told me he intended to beat Mortimer."

Holmes scoffs at your suggestion. "Thus, a poacher translated his desire to beat Mortimer into a desire to shoot him, and to shoot him in a manner that would maximize his chance of being captured and minimize the chance of seriously wounding Mortimer? Come, come, young man; that is a foolish conclusion." You blush deeply at Holmes' pointed criticism. *Turn to 225.*

431

The path through the woods suddenly opens into a broad field. A line of haystacks crosses the field, and you quickly notice that some of them have various targets attached to them. Redruth — who is the Colonel's groundskeeper — Beach, and several other servants are waiting at the edge of the field. While Beach prepares a pleasant picnic lunch for everyone, you notice that Redruth inspects a number of rifles. Presumably there will be a shooting contest before lunch.

"Given the questionable skills of some competitors," Miss Dunlop begins, "we feel it is safer to attach the first targets to the broadest haystacks in all Yorkshire. They should be able to stop even the wildest shots, even those of my beloved." She smiles at Harris, who appears uncomfortable. The guests are a bit hesitant to begin this contest, but finally Miss Dunlop takes a rifle herself and after aiming and squeezing the trigger, hits the edge of the biggest target. In turn, everyone else but Harris hits at least a corner of the target. Living up to his reputation, Harris sends bits of hay flying from the top of the stack. Redruth, who had moved off far to the side while Harris shot, indicates that the target on the stack nearby is the new focus of contention.

When your turn comes, you feel far less confident of your ability, even though no one else has missed completely. *Pick a number and add your Athletics bonus:*

• *If 2-7, turn to 284.*
• *If 8-12, turn to 553.*

432

As the men break into different groups, you avoid getting trapped in a corner by Leaf and seek out the company of Robert Harris. You talk of the various events of the upcoming weekend, the wonders of the house, and then comment: "As modest as my own business is at this time, I seldom gave the opportunity to pass such a weekend of luxury. But I can tell that you are well-accustomed to it, Mr. Harris." ***Pick a number*** *and add your Communication bonus:*

- *If 2-6,* ***turn to 574.***
- *If 7-11,* ***turn to 291.***
- *If 12,* ***turn to 549.***

433

"Well, then," Watson continues, chuckling at your reference, "does anyone arouse your suspicions? Most of the guests seem to me to be just what one would expect at such a gathering. I am a little surprised that Foxx should linger so near his former fiance, but there is no evidence that he is anyhting but a scorned suitor. Dr. Cunningham certainly is a good chap." Watson chuckles, recalling their duel at the billiards table. "Trust me; you learn whether a man is square or not when you play a ninety minute billiards match with him, when every shot is crucial to your success. And Grayson, the solicitor, is a respected man in his profession. You could not suspect him for a moment, could you?"

- *If you checked Deduction 3,* ***turn to 603.***
- *Otherwise,* ***turn to 424.***

434

"Is that the door into the gun room?" you ask the Colonel.

"Oh, yes," he answers, a little surprised. "You can see how secure it is. It would probably be easier to break through the walls than to force it open from the other side." ***Turn to 164.***

435

You complete your study of the library furniture and stand in the middle of the room, baffled. You have not learned anything from examining the furniture. ***Turn to 106.***

436

As the Mortimers and Snead turn away from you, you seek out the Colonel. He is standing with a plump, red-faced man of thirty years drinking brandy, rather than tea. The Colonel presents him as Mr. Hunter Foxx, son of a former commander of the Yorkshire Lights. "So you have met our Canadian ally," Foxx says in a nasty tone of voice. "It is well for us that our friend Snead is here for only three weeks more, or England might become a colony of Canada."

The Colonel attempts to cover this remark with a joke, but it fails miserably. The Colonel adds: "Now, Hunter, he only took what you had lost already. Take it like a man."

Their comments are something of a mystery to you.

• *If you ask about their comments, **turn to 268**.*
• *Otherwise, **turn to 471**.*

"I have no other proof," you admit. "I do not think any of the other suspects could have committed the crime."

"That is a very inadequate proof," Holmes says sharply. "If you wish to make a career as a detective, you must investigate much more carefully. Accusations based on such shaky proof will eventually get you into a great deal of trouble."

You sigh deeply, knowing that the harsh comments are justified. There must be more evidence you might have uncovered.

• *If you want to investigate the case again, **turn to the Prologue.***

• *If you want an explanation from Holmes, **turn to 119.***

438

"You've only been with us for two months?" you ask in a surprised tone. "Well, there must be truth to descriptions of the energy of the colonists. You've not only carried out your business, you will carry away one of our fairest ladies." You bow slightly to Miss Mortimer. "How did you manage such a conquest so quickly?" ***Pick a number*** *and add your Communication bonus:*

• *If 2-8, turn to 454.*

• *If 9-12, turn to 474.*

Holmes glances about, taking in all of you, then begins to explain the theft. "Colonel, your niece Ellen stole the eagle." He gestures for silence as the shocked gentleman rises to his feet to protest. "I have established a chain of clues, sir; do not protest until you hear them. The thief left a trace of greyish mud on the ladder in the library—your niece ran through mud of that same color. She had the keys to unlock the padlock, and she was the only person who had the opportunity. Neither Mr. Snead nor Mr. Foxx had time to steal the bird on their way upstairs. I was able to deduce that the thief was probably not overly strong, which would match the young lady's physique. Also, the thief obviously knew the house very well, a fact which points at her. And she had the opportunity to carry out the crime. Miss Dunlop was alone for a few minutes after she fixed the room for Mortimer, before he was brought back to the house."

"But she has no reason to steal it!" the Colonel protests, purple with rage. "She would not know how to sell it even if she wanted to."

"'Steal' may be the wrong term to use," Holmes answers smoothly. "Hide might be better, as shown by where she placed it. Distressed that her friend's wedding would be stopped by this shooting, she hoped that the disappearance of the eagle would require that everyone remain here until the matter was settled. I am surprised that Watson did not guess the answer at once. He is more expert than I at the romantic workings of the female mind." Watson blushes a little, but does not try to reply. ***Turn to 142.***

440

You find the Colonel in a corner of the library, trying to read a London paper. He is obviously upset by the day's events; the newspaper trembles in his hand. He glances at you, then asks: "Have you found a motive for the shooting?"

"I have not, " you admit, "but there is one aspect of the case I want to examine with you. Do you know any reason why anyone, especially Grayson or Harris, might wish to prevent the Mortimer-Snead marriage? That may have been the object of the crime." *Check Decision 15.* **Pick a number** *and add your Communication bonus: (Subtract 2 if you have checked Decision 16 and/or 17.)*

- *If 2-6,* **turn to 508.**
- *If 7-12,* **turn to 362.**

441

"I no longer suspect Harris," you say, surprising your cousin. "I have learned that the man has a large private income and will inherit great wealth. He wouldn't be fool enough to ruin himself and his reputation by perpetrating such a risky theft, would he?" **Turn to 193.**

442

You wonder whether you should examine anything else in Foxx's room.

- *If you checked Clue AA,* **turn to 118.**
- *Otherwise,* **turn to 575.**

443

"I do not know who stole the eagle," you admit with some shame. "My evidence is incomplete in the matter."

"Well, at least you are honest enough to admit your failure," the Colonel mutters, flustrated. "Do you know who took it, Mr. Holmes?"

- *If you want to investigate the case again,* **turn to the Prologue.**
- *If you want Holmes' explanation,* **turn to 439.**

The two of you move very carefully through the woods, trying to quietly approach the site of the noise. As you come to a small clearing, the moon emerges from behind a large cloud.

Across the clearing a small man is bent down, doing something amid the bushes. "A poacher!" Mortimer cries in an outraged voice. The man leaps to his feet and runs into the woods. With a cry, Mortimer gives chase, you on his heels. *Pick a number* and add your *Athletics bonus:*

• *If 2-8, turn to 232.*
• *If 9-12, turn to 461.*

445

You come to the point in the woods where you can intercept Grayson. To your surprise, you see him turn away from the path to town and plunge deeper into the woods, following a direction that leads back toward the house. Wondering what he is doing, you must decide whether or not to continue following him. *Check Clue Q.*

• *If you follow him,* **turn to 226.**
• *If you return to the house,* **turn to 200.**

Dr. Cunningham considers your question, then shakes his head. "The very question makes no sense to me," he says. "I do not know of any reason why someone would attempt to block the wedding, and I do not see any connection between the wedding and the shooting. I am afraid that I cannot help you," he concludes, turning back to the billiard table. You leave him there as you decide what to do next.

- *If you have not checked Decision 15 and wish to talk to Colonel Dunlop,* ***turn to 440.***
- *If you have not checked Decision 17 and wish to talk to Captain Leaf,* ***turn to 532.***
- *If you do not want to talk to either of them,* ***turn to 349.***

As breakfast ends, you hear the sounds of a carriage outside; Beach jumps to open the front door to an older couple. Susan Mortimer fairly flies from the dining room to hug them, and you realize that they must be her parents, up for the day to watch the duel. As you go into a sitting room, Beach brings you a letter that came in the morning mail. To your delight, you see it is from Mr. Holmes. You settle down in a quiet corner to read it.

> *Dear Sir:*
>
> *I have settled the other matter in the southwest. Having some leisure, I will be in Gunston this afternoon to pursue my researches into old charters. I would be pleased if you and Watson would join me for supper.*
>
> *Holmes*

When you get the chance, you show Watson the note. He is delighted.

"Good for Holmes!" he says, shaking his head in admiration. "The man settles two cases that baffled the police for a fortnight in one evening! I shall never hear the end of it."

Quickly, you tell Beach that you will sup out. In turn, he informs you that the Colonel wishes to see you in his study. The Colonel greets you warmly, thanking you for your efforts. "I want to make it clear," he adds, "that I hope you will watch the duel this morning. I feared you might feel it your duty to remain at the house. I can guarantee that no one would attempt such a theft in broad daylight. Aside from that, Beach and most of the servants will be up here, and the other guests will be at the duel."

"All the guests?" you ask.

"All but two," the Colonel replies, eyeing you warily. "Mr. Grayson is going into Gunston to send a telegram and take to care of some business matter, while Mr. Harris wishes to stay behind in his room and catch up on his correspondence. Actually," the Colonel notes, softly confiding, "both said they would feel like intruders at a function so closely connected to the Yorkshire Lights, but in that, they are mistaken. I definitely want you to see it." The man's passion for the upcoming event is almost palpable.

• *If you go to observe the duel, **turn to 415.***
• *Otherwise, **turn to 561.***

448

You begin to tell the others about the puff of smoke, then decide not to say anything. Something very puzzling is happening. You might have a better chance of solving the puzzle if you observe the others for a moment or two. ***Turn to 159.***

449

You feel bloated after the huge dinner. Perhaps a walk in the cool evening breezes would make you more comfortable.

You walk outside, politely avoiding the area where Harris and Miss Dunlop are walking together. The warm summer evening is everything you might imagine: the breeze is fresh, and trees and flowers fill the air with a pleasant fragrance. Your wanderings lead you into the wood that covers much of the Colonel's land. ***Pick a number** and add your Observation bonus:*

• *If 2-6, **turn to 413.***
• *If 7-12, **turn to 534.***

450

There is one more entrance to the library — the door from the gun room. From the Colonel's description, you know that it is secured in the same manner as is the well-protected upstairs door. You wonder if it is worth the time and risk to examine it.

• *If you go to the gun room,* ***turn to 530.***
• *Otherwise,* ***turn to 410.***

451

The Colonel is disappointed that you have not discovered Grayson's motive, but he mentions that he will take care of matters. Later that day, you and the other guests are told that Grayson has been forced to return to London due to 'a family emergency.' Several weeks later, you learn the motive for the shooting. ***Turn to 462.***

452

"You must discover who has a strong motive to stop the wedding," Holmes says. "If you can discover that person, you will have your gunman."

"How shall I proceed?" you ask.

"I can suggest two methods," Holmes answers. "You might consult the records in the local town hall, to see if there are any documents, wills or trusts, that would be affected by the marriage. Or, you may wish to talk with Colonel Dunlop or some of his more knowledgeable guests. Good hunting, at any rate."

• *If you visit the town hall,* ***turn to 396.***
• *If you return to Eagle Towers,* ***turn to 273.***

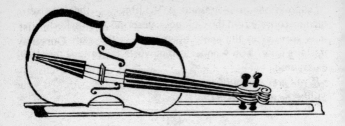

453

Fortunately, you have spent time working in the public records office in London, and you know how to search for the information you need. You begin to consult the indices of the local wills and trusts funds, and find one that lists documents by beneficiary. Only one document mentions the name Mortimer; the will of a Robert Murphy of Eagle Towers, a document filed more than sixty years ago. The clerk fetches the will and its accompanying documents; the papers clarify the case immensely. If Snead and Susan Mortimer, as descendants of the original duellists, marry, they will inherit Murphy's wealth. Grayson, the solicitor, is sole trustee for the estate. The file includes papers prepared by him, showing that he has invested the estate in a railroad he is developing. The information triggers your memory, and understanding follows. If Grayson were forced to withdraw the capital to pay off the inheritance, the railroad would fail and Grayson would be ruined. Obviously, he has a strong motive to stop the wedding. As he was not at the duel, he could have been the hidden gunman. Accompanied by Watson, you hurry back to Eagle Towers and explain the matter to Colonel Dunlop. He arranges for Grayson to leave immediately. Pleased to have thwarted the crime, you happily attend the wedding two weeks later. But even amid the good cheer of that ceremony, one thought teases you — what will you investigate next? A murder? Perhaps a kidnapping? You can hardly wait to begin! The End

454

Snead's handsome face darkens at the question, and Miss Mortimer looks slightly shocked. Watson coughs into his fist, perhaps signaling you that you have gone too far. "Ours may seem a backward country to you, sir," Snead says in a hard voice, "but we have the dignity to avoid casually discussing personal matters with every chance acquaintance." To your relief, he turns away. *Turn to 436.*

455

You manage to stimulate Harris into talking about his life, and though he does delve into details, he seems to follow the routine of the idle rich: a life of hunting and week-long parties at county houses. It seems that Harris does not work; you wonder whether he is wealthy or merely skilled at evoking invitations from the wealthy. Finally, a joke by Miss Dunlop presents you with an opening to ask his opinion of the jewel thefts.

• If you ask Harris about the thefts, *turn to 368.*
• Otherwise, *turn to 590.*

456

Accompanied by Watson, Jackson and Colonel Dunlop, you cross the clearing to the woods, searching for evidence of the hidden gunman. It will not be easy, as you only have a general idea of where the marksman stood. *Turn to 404.*

457

You watch both uniformed men, listening as Captain Leaf calls: "Ready! One!" Smoke erupts from Mortimer's gun as the shot explodes. "Two!...Three!" Snead fires, having brought his weapon up slowly and smoothly. Then chaos overtakes the anticipated scene. As if actually shot, Mortimer cries in pain, grabbing at his neck as he collapses. A woman screams, and the men's astonished shouts add to the confusion. *Pick a number* and add your Observation bonus: (Add 3 if you checked Clue S.)

• If 2-11, *turn to 159.*
• If 12, *turn to 501.*

Grayson displays the sharpness of the legal mind, quickly and convincingly explaining that he saw you sneak through the woods, and acted just in time to prevent you from shooting Mortimer. He makes your charges against him seem foolish. "But why would he do it?" a bewildered Mortimer asks. "I've only known the fellow for two days."

"You know what low fellows these investigators are," Grayson answers, leaping to his cue. "He had satisfied himself that the Colonel's fears for the safety of the eagle were groundless, and he thus invented another 'crime' in order to continue taking advantage of the Colonel's extraordinary hospitality."

In spite of Watson's vigorous protests, Colonel Dunlop believes the solicitor. "Thank you, Grayson," he says, shaking the cad's hand. "You have prevented a most unpleasant incident. You and Dr. Watson," he says, turning to you, his face grim, "must leave my land at once. Beach will pack your things and send them to the inn in Gunston; I will not have either of you on my land a moment longer." You have no choice but to obey the Colonel's orders. With Watson's assistance, you pack and leave Eagle Towers in forlorn silence.

Later that evening, you are still humiliated and embarrassed when you meet Holmes for dinner at the Gunston Inn. "It is unfortunate that your investigation ended in such a disheartening manner," the detective says, his eyes on the door, "but you can at least take comfort in your prevention of the shooting. That is the most important part of our work, sir: preventing crime."

"What I cannot understand is why Grayson wished to shoot Mortimer," Watson says. "I saw no signs of enmity between them. Why?" Holmes glances your way, giving you the first chance to answer the question.

- *If you checked Clue L and either Clue K or N, **turn to 427**.*
- *If you checked Clue K or N, but not Clue L, **turn to 318**.*
- *Otherwise, **turn to 354**.*

459

You apply all your skills to the heavy padlock but cannot open it. The gate remains closed. You feel satisfied that no one can enter the library from this side. ***Turn to 393.***

460

"Before you name the thief," Holmes continues, "have you discovered where the golden bird is hidden?"
- *If you say it is hidden upstairs,* ***turn to 556.***
- *If you say it is behind books in the library,* ***turn to 576.***
- *If you say it is hidden in the dumbwaiter,* ***turn to 166.***
- *If you say it was passed to someone outside,* ***turn to 121.***

461

Leaping small bushes and ducking low limbs, you and Mortimer chase the little but quick man through the woods. Though the alledged poacher passes among the trees like a will-o'-the-wisp, you draw closer to him. Mortimer is coming from another direction, and as the man hesitates, you dive for him. Your tackle knocks the legs out from under him, and he doesn't try to escape. Together, you and Mortimer dragh him to the house to face the Colonel and explain what he was doing. ***Turn to 360.***

You eventually learn the motive from a note that Mrs. Snead (formerly Susan Mortimer) sends to Holmes.

Dear Mr. Holmes:

Lacking his address, I cannot write to your associate, Mr. Hurley. Therefore, I would be pleased if you should be so kind as to show him this note, which contains the reason for the terrible assault upon my brother, John. After our marriage, Robert and I were informed that we were entitled to a large inheritance, left to the first members of our families to wed. Mr. Grayson was sole trustee for the estate and told us he would need a few weeks to deliver us the money, as it was tied up in a long-term investment. While shocked to learn that Mr. Grayson would fire at my brother to retain control of the money, we granted him the time, as it seemed there was no other choice. My husband investigated his company and decided that the money should be left there, as it is a prime investment. Mr. Grayson's remorse was intense, as he realized that there was no need for him to behave so abominably. Thank your friend for his help, Mr. Holmes. Even if he did not uncover the solution to the mystery, he at least learned enough to preserve our engagement. We leave for Canada next week.

Affectionately, Susan Snead

"Ironic, isn't it Holmes?" Watson comments. "Grayson risked ruin though he was in no danger at all."

"That is the way of all criminals, is it not, Watson?" Holmes replies. "Their guilt breeds fear, and fear will always betray a man in the end. Such lower emotions interfere with the logical consideration of a question necessary to success in any endeavour."

As Holmes and Watson continue to discuss the case, you wonder what peculiar crime will inspire your next investigation. The End

463

As you stand and listen in the empty library, the eerie quiet begins to unsettle your nerves. You hear a noise coming from behind a couch and the bookcases. Could it be some other intruder shifting positions as he watches you? It may not be safe to stay here now.

• If you investigate the noise, **turn to 151.**
• If you leave the library, **turn to 319.**

464

"But you must know why Grayson shot Mortimer," Holmes says slowly, as if emphasizing his superior powers of deduction, "although you obviously do not recognize what you know. You told me that Grayson was trustee for the will which will pay a large sum of money to Snead and Susan Mortimer when they marry. If they had believed Snead to be responsible for their son's brush with death, the Mortimers would certainly have banned the wedding at once. I happen to know that Grayson's enterprises, while sound concerns, are terribly strapped for cash. Obviously, he must have tied up the capital from the trust fund in them, so that paying it to the happy couple would ruin him. Thus, he developed a desperate scheme to escape his dilemma, which at least did not result in murder. You did well to assemble the evidence you found, even if you did not use it perfectly."

Sparked by Holmes' compliments, you return to Eagle Towers and explain the case to Colonel Dunlop. Enraged, the Colonel orders Grayson to leave the house very suddenly (due to a "family emergency"), and the weekend continues to its end. Although you try to throw yourself heartily into the entertainments, you wonder when you will have the chance to investigate another mystery. The challenge cannot come too soon! The End

465

The dumbwaiter proves to be another blind alley. You wonder where else you might uncover a useful clue. **Turn to 224.**

466

The tied ropes strike you as being a very odd thing, but you are not sure what it means. You decide not to reveal your discovery until you have uncovered other information. *Check Decision 25. Turn to 224.*

467

You examine the door and find it locked; the inside bolts apparently remained fastened. It seems that Miss Mortimer did nothing to the door. Soon you and Watson join the other guests in the sitting room for an aperitif. *Turn to 277.*

468

As the train carries you west and beyond the furthest reaches of London, Watson pulls a book from his pocket and settles himself more comfortably in his seat. He seems to take no notice of the pleasant, green countryside rolling by at a speeding glance.

"What are you reading, John?" you ask, curious.

He shows you the cover of the book. "It is a novel, *Micah Clark*, by my friend, Dr. Conan Doyle. He has a gift for historical romance. This one is set in the days of Monmouth's Revolution." He pauses, then adds: "I have one or two things you might want to read." Your cousin offers you two pamphlets. One is entitled "The Art of Jewel Theft," written by a man Holmes sent to Dartmoor. The other is "A History of the Yorkshire Light Artillery."

- *If you read "The Art of Jewel Theft,"* **turn to 137.**
- *If you read "A History of the Yorkshire Light Artillery,"* **turn to 347.**
- *If you take a nap,* **turn to 503.**

You and Mortimer talk quietly for a few minutes; then you turn the conversation to his sister's wedding. "Yes, yes, Snead seems like a good enough fellow," Mortimer admits. "Of course, no man is really good enough for my sister, but Snead seems to suit her. I only wish there were more time before the wedding."

"I understand that Snead must return to Canada soon," you offer.

"That's true," Mortimer replies thoughtfully. "I wish they would stay in England, where she belongs, but the girl must be free to make her own choices." He sighs deeply. ***Turn to 210.***

470

You then realize that Colonel Dunlop traveled with the group and could not have crossed the mud. ***Turn to 495.***

You are relieved when the Colonel tells Foxx that he must introduce you to the other guests. The remaining two guests stand talking in a corner. The taller man is obviously an officer or ex-officer, a stiff disciplined-looking man of thirty-five or so. The other man is short and slender, with a lined face and thinning hair. Dunlop introduces the tall fellow as Lieutenant Jackson and the other as Thomas Grayson, a solicitor from York. As you chat with them, you wonder why the solicitor is here. He appears to be no more than a casual acquaintance of the Colonel.

"My, we are a mixed group," you say, laughing nervously. "I feel less out of place than I did at first. But what brings you here, Mr. Grayson?" you ask.

"Thomas is my guest," Lieutenant Jackson interjects, puffing out his chest. "He was kind enough to make a special trip to my place at South Riding Monday in order to bring me several inportant papers. He then was forced to stay over, in order to review them with me. Naturally, when Colonel Dunlop came by my home Tuesday afternoon, he insisted that Thomas join us for the weekend — they have known each other for many years." As the conversation turns to other topics, you consider the Lieutenant's comments for a moment.
Pick a number and add your Intuition bonus:
• If 2-6, *turn to 315.*
• If 7-12, *turn to 374.*

472

You then realize that anyone would have noticed Snead if he had left to group to run through the mud. *Turn to 495.*

473

You begin to examine the library. A long, polished wooden ladder leans against the mantle where the eagle once rested. Obviously, the thief used it to get at the golden bird. *Pick a number* and add your Observation bonus:
• If 2-7, *turn to 221.*
• If 8-12, *turn to 181.*

474

Snead's handsome face darkens, then he suddenly laughs. "I think, sir," he says, "that my success shows that I am an extraordinarily fortunate man; it has little to do with energy or any other good quality, I fear. It so happened that when I first visited Colonel Dunlop with letters of introduction, he took me to a party at the Mortimers. There had been some family dispute, and in return, I believe that Susan was seeking to shock her parents. A Canadian fiance fitted her needs, and I wouldn't let her break the engagement once it was announced. I am nothing if not dogged, sir."

At first, Susan looks outraged; then she bursts into a fit of laughter. "Come along, Robert," she says, "you must find me some more tea or I shall never speak to you again." *Turn to 436*.

475

When you consider his movements, you realize that Leaf could not possibly have run through the mud. *Turn to 495*.

Trying to be as thorough as possible, you open the dumb-waiter and see only the ropes that work it. Curious, you tug at them, and find that they will not move at all. "The dumbwaiter seems to be completely broken," you comment. "I cannot budge the ropes."

"I'm not surprised," the Colonel says. "It has been useless for years." ***Pick a number*** and add your *Observation bonus*:
• *If 2-8,* ***turn to 465.***
• *If 9-12,* ***turn to 601.***

477

You now realize that Jackson would have called attention to himself if he had left the group to run through the mud. Such was not the case. ***Turn to 495.***

478

You stand and watch as the doctors supervise the servants, who gingerly lift Mortimer onto the stretcher. The lieutenant seems to be dazed by his injury. There are plenty of hands to carry the cot towards the house. You manage to overhear Snead tell Colonel Dunlop that he ought to leave on the evening train. Snead obviously realizes that his continued presence would be an embarassment. Once at the house, Beach leads the bearers into a ground floor bedroom which has been prepared for Mortimer. Dr. Cunningham quickly takes charge and orders everyone except Susan Mortimer out of the room. As you and the others leave, you notice that Snead, Foxx, Jackson and Leaf are missing from the group.

As your group passes the library, the Colonel glances in, gasps and curses. "My God!" he cries, aghast, "the Eagle is gone!" Everyone crowds towards the hall entrance to look, but you get there first. With the Colonel's agreement, you ask Watson to keep everyone else out of the room while you investigate. From outside you hear Beach comment that the eagle cannot have been gone long, for he had gone through the library recently himself. You study the scene, and try to decide what to do. *Pick a number* and add your Intuition bonus:

• *If 2-7, turn to 473.*
• *If 8-12, turn to 275.*

479

You kneel by the door and carefully check the wax you left joining the door to the frame. You find that the wax is unbroken; therefore, no one had used this door since you fixed the wax last night. *Turn to 567.*

"Money was the motive," you explain to the excited crowd, "the source of many a crime. Grayson needs money very badly, as he is trustee for an estate that will be paid to Mr. Snead and Miss Mortimer if they marry. Undoubtedly he has already committed that money to some project. Withdrawing it to pay what is due the couple would ruin him."

"But why shoot at me?" Mortimer asks again. "If he killed Snead, he would have stopped the wedding, too."

Snead bows, obviously eager to be considered an equally important target. "I doubt that Grayson wanted to kill anyone," Dr. Cunningham suggests. "He is a very fine shot. Probably, he would have fired at the same time that Snead did. If Snead appeared to have wounded you in the duel, it would have stopped the marriage." You and the others discuss the case at some length before returning to the house. That evening you and Watson go to Gunston and meet Mr. Holmes at a local inn for supper.

After eating, you explain the facts of the case to Holmes, who listens quietly, smoking his pipe. "An excellent investigation," he says when you have finished. "You are learning your craft well and took advantage of such luck as you had. I reached town yesterday evening and spent the morning at the courthouse, where I read that rather odd will. I was concerned as soon as I read it. I knew that Grayson was a guest at Eagle Towers, and that any such will could lead even a good man into temptation."

You talk further with Holmes and Watson, delighted by their compliments. Already you wonder what your next case will be. The End

When you have finished, Holmes nods slowly. Your heart races; will he agree? "You have established proof for your charge," he says slowly. "Miss Dunlop must be the person who took the eagle." *Turn to 120.*

Harris was nowhere near the patch of mud and could not have been the one who ran through it. *Turn to 495.*

483

For the moment, you have finished questioning the witnesses. Beach tells you that Harris has just returned to the house, but as with Snead and Foxx, there is little to be gained in questioning him. Either he was away from the house, as he appears to have been, or else he stole the eagle and certainly will not admit it. You consider searching individual rooms upstairs. Those of Snead, Foxx and Miss Dunlop are available for discrete inspection at the moment.

• If you search upstairs, **turn to 182**.
• Otherwise, **turn to 369**.

484

The duellists wait, standing in their places, their sides pointing toward the opponent (to reduce the target) and gun arms by their sides. 'What shall I watch during the duel?' you wonder.

• If you watch for movement in the bushes, **turn to 558**.
• If you watch Snead closely, **turn to 507**.
• If you watch Mortimer closely, **turn to 529**.
• If you watch the entire scene, **turn to 457**.

485

As you walk among the trees, you suddenly hear a faint rustling noise in the brush. You touch Mortimer's arm and signal that he should stop and listen. Almost immediately he nods — he has heard the sound too. **Turn to 444.**

486

Watson rises from the wounded man's side while Dr. Cunningham finishes bandaging the wound. You get Watson aside and whisper: "There is something I don't understand about this wound, John."

"What is that?" he asks, wiping his hand on a serving linen.

• If you think the wound was not made by a duelling pistol, **turn to 492**.
• If you think the location of the wound implies foul play, **turn to 322**.
• If you are certain that Sneed's gun was not loaded, **turn to 573**.

Colonel Dunlop concludes his discussion of the weapons, then points to a door in the back wall. "That door leads to the terrace outside," he explains, "but it should not be a concern to you. It is both locked and barred at night." You nod in understanding and make way for the Colonel as he leads you back to the library. No one else is in the room. "I asked my niece to take everyone out to look at the horses," the Colonel explains. "I wanted to allow you to look over the security of this room without interruption." You begin with the main entrances, noting that there is a sliding grate which closes each of the two archways. A padlock and chain secure them. The high mantle over the fireplace forms a wide shelf perfectly suited to display of a variety of artwork. The Colonel mentions that he usually sets a bust of Wellington there, which is only removed when the Eagle is brought out for the reunion. You then turn your attention to the Eagle. The golden bird is mounted on a heavy wooden base, which has polished steel rings at each corner. Chains run from the back of the shelf through these rings on either side and are secured by padlocks at the front. *Pick a number* and add your Observation bonus:

• *If 2-7, turn to 164.*
• *If 8-12, turn to 384.*

"I have uncovered no clues indicating that someone hates Mortimer enough to shoot him," you admit. "He seemed to have no serious problems with any other guests." *Turn to 270.*

Your careful examination of the ladder is worthwhile. On one of the lower rungs, you find a trace of greyish-colored mud. You try to remember just where you have seen mud of that color. *Check Clue Z. Pick a number* and add your *Observation bonus:*

• *If 2-6, turn to 372.*
• *If 7-12, turn to 520.*

490

You consider what next to do. Everyone is gathered in the drawing room except for John and Susan Mortimer and Dr. Cunningham, who are in Mortimer's bedroom.

Above the nervous hubbub, the Colonel calls for order. "I must have your attention!" he calls, and everyone is quiet. "We have a thief amongst us." He pauses to allow comment, then continues. "I ask your kind indulgence. Please make no plans to leave until the thief of the eagle is revealed. Thank you." Everyone looks more than a little put out and quite impatient.

The Colonel motions you to his side to whisper: "It would be wise to complete your investigation as soon as possible."
• *If you checked Clue AA, **turn to 333.***
• *Otherwise, **turn to 196.***

491

The idea of Watson as the thief makes you laugh to yourself. You must remember to tell him the story. ***Turn to 495.***

492

"Even if the gun were loaded, a duelling pistol could not wound a man in that way, not firing from such an angle," you say eagerly.

"No, cousin, you are wrong," Watson replies. "The bullet just grazed him — any gun could have inflicted that wound." ***Turn to 103.***

493

It is obvious that Dr. Cunningham did not abandon the stretcher to run through the mud. ***Turn to 495.***

494

The spinning apples bring a mercifully quick end to the contest. Grayson smashes his with one shot, while you and the others miss. You join the ladies and the other men in congratulating the solicitor on his marksmanship. Soon, everyone begins to discuss lunch eagerly. It has been a full and busy morning. ***Turn to 345.***

495

The identity of the person leaving the prints remains a mystery. *Turn to 568.*

496

You consider talking to Lieutenant Jackson, to see if he noticed anything.
• *If you talk to Jackson,* **turn to 498.**
• *Otherwise,* **turn to 180.**

497

"Actually, my question regards a private matter, Captain," you explain. "It looks as though the shooting today might shatter the engagement between Mr. Snead and Miss Mortimer. Would anyone benefit from that sad occurrence?"

Leaf laughs heartily. "Why, any free man might benefit from Susan Mortimer becoming available once again," he jokes, "but I know of no one who would gain by ruining the wedding. Many benefits would accrue, in fact." *Pick a number and add your Intuition bonus:*
• *If 2-7,* **turn to 251.**
• *If 8-12,* **turn to 227.**

498

Jackson comes in and sits in the chair. The brandy has relaxed him considerably. "I understand you went straight to the drawing room," you begin. "Did you hear anything from the library while you were there, before the others came in and you learnred the eagle was gone?"

Jackson shakes his head. "You know Captain Leaf," he says with a smile. "If you were alone with him, would you have heard anything in an adjoining room, anything short of a cannon?" He laughs and cannot give you any other useful information. *Turn to 180.*

499

"No one except for you and the servants," she answers, smiling. "And you came out of the drawing room, not the library." *Turn to 526.*

500

You try to sort through the indices to local documents and look through some of the papers themselves, but cannot find any way to identify who might benefit from the breakup of the Snead-Mortimer engagement. You return to Eagle Towers, hoping that someone can provide the missing clue. ***Turn to 273.***

501

As you watch, a puff of smoke rises from the woods across the clearing. Another gunman fired at the same time that Snead discharged his pistol! What is happening? *Check Clue T.*

• *If you tell everyone of the other gunman,* ***turn to 276.***
• *Otherwise,* ***turn to 448.***

502

You talk with Harris for a while longer, until he says politely: "Excuse me, please. I promised my fiance that I would walk with her this evening, and the time is flying by." As Harris leaves the library, you wonder what to do next. Captain Leaf seeks someone to talk to, but you could take a walk outside, or go upstairs to your room.

• *If you talk to Leaf,* ***turn to 127.***
• *If you go outside,* ***turn to 308.***
• *If you go to your room,* ***turn to 578.***

503

Neither pamphlet appeals to you. As Watson buries his head in his book, you lay your head back and drift off to sleep. Why worry about the case until you can arrive at the scene?

You awaken from a pleasant dream as the train slows and the brakes hiss and grind. Looking over at your cousin, you see Watson putting away his novel. ***Turn to 329.***

504

The locks and bolts appear to be set the way they were last night, but you cannot prove that some skillful burglar did not exit by the door. However, you are certain of one fact — the man would have to be a miracle worker to bolt the door so securely from the other side. *Turn to 567.*

505

You wait to hear Holmes' evaluation of your proof, delighted to see the great detective smile. "You have done very well," Holmes says. "You have built a solid case. There can be no doubt that Miss Dunlop took the eagle." *Turn to 120.*

506

"I have no other physical evidence," you admit. "However, the thief must have known the house very well, and Miss Dunlop would, of course."

• *If you checked Deduction 19,* **turn to 325.**
• *Otherwise,* **turn to 481.**

507

You watch Snead closely as Captain Leaf calls "Ready! One!" Mortimer's pistol fires. Then Leaf continues: "Two!...Three!" Snead brings his gun up and fires. *Pick a number* and add your Observation Bonus:

• *If 2-8,* **turn to 596.**
• *If 9-12,* **turn to 205.**

508

As you ask your question, you realize you have been too obvious in your hunt for a suspect and have not acted with the necessary discretion. The elder Mortimers and Grayson angrily approach and demand to know how you dare ask such personal questions. They quickly transfer their anger to Colonel Dunlop.

"Who is this person?" asks Mr. Mortimer, almost stuttering with rage. "Is it your custom, Colonel, to include a professional busybody on your guest list?" The Colonel is obviously upset at the disturbance and pointedly suggests that you leave in the morning.

• *If you checked Clue X, **turn to 353**.*
• *Otherwise, **turn to 124**.*

509

You go to work on the lock again, trying to relock it. You find that this is an entirely different operation from unfastening the lock. ***Pick a number** and add your Artifice bonus: (Add 2 if you have the skeleton keys):*

• *If 2-8, **turn to 162**.*
• *If 9-12, **turn to 104**.*

510

When Leaf smiles again at a burst of angry words from the card game, you dare to ask: "Captain, you seem to be enjoying the argument. That seems an odd reaction, no?"

The Captain leads you from the billiard room and into another parlour. "Sit down, young man," he says genially, "and I will tell you something." You settle into a comfortable chair, wondering what kind of marathon tale you shall be forced to endure.

"You see, sir," Captain Leaf begins, "the high point of these reunions, at least to my mind, is the recreation of the old Snead-Mortimer duel. Yes," he adds, before you can interrupt, "young Snead and Mortimer are the great grandsons of the original duelists. Their ancestors faced each other in a duel one week before the Battle of Waterloo. As you must have surmised, it was a bitter dispute. Tomorrow, the great grandsons will recreate those roles, and I am very pleased to see them show some temper. Their anger will make tomorrow's event more... realistic."

"What caused the original duel?" you ask. "Outraged honour," the captain replies. "Snead wished to marry Mortimer's sister, who was only sixteen. As Snead had already buried one wife and had a son, Mortimer felt the match was inappropriate and blocked it. When they fought, Mortimer fired quickly and missed. Snead, renowned as a dead shot, deliberately aimed wide. However, as they exchanged courtesies afterward, it was obvious they had not forgotten their hatred."

"Hardly proper was it?" you mutter. "No, not at all," Leaf replies with a bit of a chuckle. "In fact, if not for events at Waterloo, the duel would be a blot on one battery's history rather than one of its shining moments. The glory of their honour was not dimmed by the mortal wounds that both suffered before the terrible day was done. After the battle, Snead's sister emigrated to Canada, taking the orphaned boy with her. Mortimer also left behind a son. And now, their heirs meet for the first time since that valiant day. They will recreate the original duel for us, on the seventy-fifth anniversary of the original. Snead loves Mortimer's sister, as happened before. What a surprise they shall receive on their wedding day," the captain says somewhat mysteriously, chuckling to himself. *Check Clue D.* **Pick a number** *and add your Intuition bonus:*
• *If 2-7,* **turn to 373.**
• *If 8-12,* **turn to 219.**

511

"I think she stole it at the behest of her fiance, Harris," you say. "The young man must need money and misused her love to lead the young lady into this shocking action."

"Nonsense!" a furious Holmes snaps. "Lestrade at his worst would not propose so preposterous a notion. There is no evidence to support it, and Mr. Harris is a rich and honest young man." **Turn to 138.**

512

You walk down the hall to Foxx's room and stop outside the door. 'Have I any reason to search it?' you wonder.
• *If you search Foxx's room,* **turn to 285.**
• *Otherwise,* **turn to 575.**

513

"Thomas Snead stole the eagle," you conclude. "He left the group as soon as they returned to the house, and his movements cannot be accounted for with any exactness."

"And how would he have done this?" Holmes asks, clearly skeptical. As he blows smoke rings to the ceiling, you see your dreams of detection dissipating with them. "While it is true that the key to his trunk would also open the padlocks, I doubt that he would have run upstairs, gotten the key, run back downstairs, taken the eagle, and returned upstairs in the time available to him. In addition, how would he benefit from the theft? Even if he managed to smuggle the eagle out of the house, he would not know how to sell it, and would not have dared trying to leave the country with such a well-known object in his luggage." *Turn to 540.*

514

You edge along the molding towards the mantle. Already you are beginning to have more respect for Colonel Dunlop's security arrangements; then your right foot slips off the molding! Although you manage to choke a scream, you fall heavily to the library floor, knocking over a small table covered with small objects that smash on the floor.

Painfully bruised, you take several minutes to arise. You notice that Watson has prudently hidden behind the drawing room curtains by the time that Colonel Dunlop, Mortimer, Beach and several servants rush into the room. Blushing to your toes, you explain your actions to the Colonel, uncertain whether he is outraged or amused at your actions.

The Colonel clears his throat. "Our young friend was testing the security of the eagle, as I asked him to do. All is well. Please return to your rooms, and good night!"

As the others make their way to their rooms, you painfully climb the stairs to your bedroom, where Watson tends your injuries.

"You will be stiff and sore for several days," your cousin warns. "You need rest, dear boy." *Reduce your Athletics bonus by 1 for the remainder of this case. Turn to 235.*

None of the shoes in the closet is marked with the mud, but as you turn away from them, you notice another pair partially hidden by the bed. You pick them up and see traces of the mud on the bottoms and sides. So Miss Dunlop ran through the grey mud — could she have stolen the eagle? Why? *Check Clue FF.* **Turn to 146.**

516

"I think I can reason through the case," you say slowly, gathering your thoughts. Watson and Holmes lean nearer, listening intently. "Mr. Grayson, the solicitor, is sole trustee of an enormous estate, the capital of which will be paid to the couple when they marry. If he were using — or misusing — the money in his own business affairs, he might find it disastrous to be forced to part with it."

Holmes nods, his face displaying satisfaction with you analysis. "Very good," he says, "I saw the will today, while looking at some other papers in the town hall. And I know that Grayson's company, the Whitby and York, needs every penny it can get. Come, let us finish our dinner; then we shall go to Eagle Towers and explain the case to the Colonel." As Holmes and Watson discuss the jewel thefts which Holmes solved in Devon and Cornwall, you eat in silence. Already you wonder what puzzle will form the basis for your next case. The End

You explain what you have seen and done to Colonel Dunlop and the others, whose mouths grow wide with horror. With Watson's strong endorsement of your character, they scorn Grayson's version of events. The rifle clutched in his hand does little to improve his credibility.

"To think that I treated you as a guest!" the Colonel shouts, his face a frightening shade of red. "Thomas Grayson, you are a disgrace! Get yourself off my property and never speak to me again! I shall have Beach pack your things and send them to your home. Be thankful that I am sparing you the scandal of a court case."

Overwhelmed by the anger of his former friends, Grayson walks away without saying a word. Amid the excited talk of all the other people, Mortimer's confused voice is loudest: "But why would he shoot at me? I had never met the man before this weekend, much less have given him cause to kill me!" The others look toward you for an explanation.

- *If you checked Clue L and either Clue K or N, **turn to 480**.*
- *If you checked Clue K or N, but not Clue L, **turn to 371**.*
- *Otherwise, **turn to 304**.*

When Foxx returned to his room, he appears to have dropped his keys and money on the little table by his bed. Among the ordinary things, you spy a small piece of metal which reminds you of a picklock you once took from a burglar you apprehended. Could it open the padlock? You cannot resist the temptation to try it. ***Pick a number** and add your Artifice bonus:*

- *If 2-7, **turn to 242**.*
- *If 8-12, **turn to 170**.*

"I saw no one except the servants," Miss Dunlop answers. "None of them was working near the library." ***Turn to 526**.*

520

You concentrate on the mud, which is a pale shade of gray. After thinking for a minute or two, you remember where you saw it. There is a patch of dirt and mud this color halfway between the house and the site of the duel. You recall how the path to the clearing curves around the mud. *Check Clue AA.* **Turn to 428.**

521

Your first step is to go up to the gallery and walk to the door to the upstairs hallway. (You can at least remove the evidence of your earlier intrusion by relocking the door.) You return down the steps, certain that there must be something useful you can do here. *Erase your check on Decision 7.* **Turn to 560.**

522

"I saw a man hiding in the edge of the woods just before the recreation of the duel," you say. "He must have fired the shot that wounded Mortimer."

"You did not see him fire the shot then?" Holmes asks, and you shake your head. "How do you know that he was not a local person who came to see the show? Seeing a man is not enough, even if it led you to a correct guess."

"But Holmes, how can you know that there was another marksman?" Watson asks. "You were not present. We were."
- If you want Holmes' explanation, **turn to 194.**
- If you want to investigate the case again, **turn to the Prologue.**

523

You come up behind the man without making a sound. He does not hear you until you are only a few feet away; then he jumps and spins around. You see that the hidden observer is the poacher, Badger Phillips.

"What are you doing here?" you ask in a harsh voice. "Speak up, man, or I shall call for the servants." *Check Clue M.*
- If you have the walking stick, **turn to 336.**
- Otherwise, **turn to 144.**

524

"Oh, I seriously doubt that Phillips has any intention of stealing the eagle," you tell Watson, who yawns. "I saw him when outside tonight and asked what he was doing. He insisted that he was looking for Mortimer, to give him a thrashing for last night's incident. I doubt that such a small-time fellow would extend his poaching to eagles." *Turn to 433*.

525

As soon as you reach Eagle Towers, Beach summons you to the Colonel's study. "Well?" Dunlop demands fiercely, "Did you find any evidence of who committed this atrocity?"

"No, I did not," you admit slowly. "The guilty party hid his trail well. We shall have to find some other means to identify him. This evening, Dr. Watson and I are dining in Gunston with Mr. Holmes. I shall lay the case before him and entertain his suggestions."

"I wish Holmes had been here today," the Colonel mutters, "but I know you will do your best. Move carefully, young man. I will not allow a scandal to spoil the entire affair for everyone." You agree to proceed tactfully, and the Colonel tells his coachman to take you into Gunston.

He leaves you outside the Gunston Arms; the first man you see in the taproom is Sherlock Holmes. *Turn to 394*.

526

You consider her answer, then ask: "And after Mortimer was carried back to the house and placed in his room?"

Miss Dunlop does not answer and appears uneasy.

You add: "Did you see anything then?" *Pick a number and add your Communication bonus:*
• *If 2-7, turn to 401.*
• *If 8-12, turn to 264.*

527

You go to the closet and examine the shoes, which appear to be clean. Either Foxx did not change his shoes when he came upstairs after the duel, or else he cleaned the shoes he was wearing. You can learn nothing from his shoes. *Turn to 575*.

Carefully you climb the rail and begin to edge along the molding. However, it takes only a few shuffling steps before you realize that you will not be able to reach the mantle safely.

"It's bloody impossible!" you whisper in frustration. Reluctantly, you return to the gallery and the main floor of the library. *Turn to 344.*

You stare at the uniformed Mortimer as Captain Leaf calls: "Ready! One!" Mortimer quickly swings his gun up and fires. As the gunshot echoes through the trees, Leaf counts "Two!...Three!", and you hear the crack of Snead's gun. To your utter amazement Mortimer cries out in pain, his hand grabbing at his neck. He spins half-around as he staggers to the ground. The women scream, the men call out in astonishment, and everyone runs to his side.

"What's happened?" Watson cries. *Turn to 159.*

Although examining the gunroom seems a waste of time, your conscience forces you to check every entrance to the library. You signal Watson to follow you toward the gun room. You stop for a moment outside the door. Was that a noise inside the gun room or merely a figment of your overactive imagination?

You signal Watson to stop, then open the door as quietly as possible. A person stands at the far end of the room, examining something with the aid of a bulls-eye lantern.

• *If you speak to the stranger, turn to 292.*
• *If you sneak up on him, turn to 215.*

You move as quietly as Holmes himself and manage to stay close to Grayson. Pleased, you wonder whether the task is worth the effort. Just as he had said, Grayson seems to be taking the most direct path to Gunston.

• *If you continue to follow him, turn to 425.*
• *If you return to the house, turn to 200.*

You find Captain Leaf in the drawing room, chatting with Jackson and Harris and renewing his lifelong friendship with the brandy decanter. You make an excuse to talk to him about the battery's history and notice that the other two leave hurriedly, after making polite excuses. Apparently you are not the only poor soul to have experienced the Captain's exhausting ability to tell a story. *Check Decision 17. Pick a number and add your Communication bonus: (Subtract 2 if you have checked Decision 15 and/or 16.)*

• *If 2-6, turn to 508.*
• *If 7-12, turn to 258.*

533

You summon Watson from the drawing room and go upstairs with him. You decide to concentrate your search of the three rooms while Watson looks through the second floor's hiding places. As Watson enters a storage closet, you pause outside Snead's room. You wonder if you can eliminate any of the suspects without a search.

• If you search Snead's room, **turn to 230.**
• Otherwise, **turn to 512.**

534

You become aware that someone is crouched in the brush at the edge of the wood, staring intently at the house. What is he doing? Discretion suggests that you leave him alone.

• If you ignore him, **turn to 413.**
• If you try to sneak up on him, **turn to 234.**

535

As you turn to pick up your clean shirt, you hear an odd, scraping noise in the hall, followed by a quickly suppressed outburst of giggling. "What was that?" you ask Watson.

"Oh, nothing," he answers, distracted by his efforts to put on his tie. "Probably the young ladies enjoying a shared secret." Watson returns his attention to his tie.

• If you see what caused the noise, **turn to 305.**
• Otherwise, **turn to 327.**

536

"So we admit that a marksman shot Mortimer," Holmes says. "That leaves one more crucial question for our friend. Consider the evidence which you have discovered and tell us who hid in the woods and shot Mortimer."

"Yes, tell us, lad!" the Colonel urges.

• If you accuse Harris, **turn to 220.**
• If you accuse Badger Phillips, **turn to 592.**
• If you accuse Grayson, **turn to 250.**

537

The firm ground, covered in many places with leaves and tall grass, defeats all your efforts to trail the sniper. After a long search, you must give up and return to the house. *Turn to 525.*

538

"No offense, Cousin, but your notes are not much help," you comment after Watson completes his summary. "The wily thief seems to take advantage of whatever opportunity he finds."

"Then we must be alert enough to offer him no opportunity whatsover," Watson answers grimly. "Too often Holmes assumes that no one else can act effectively in a case like this. We must show him how wrong he is." You ask Watson another question or two regarding his notes but learn nothing of use. *Turn to 468.*

539

Although you and the others search the bushes very carefully, you cannot pinpoint exactly where the shot came from, nor do you find any trace of the gunman. Disappointed, you return to the house. *Turn to 525.*

540

You blush, embarrassed at having accused the wrong person. You might do better if given another chance to investigate.

• *If you wish to investigate the case again,* **turn to the Prologue.**
• *If you want to hear Mr. Holmes' explanation,* **turn to 439.**

541

"I found some very solid physical evidence," you begin. "There was a bit of greyish-colored mud on the ladder in the library. I found mud of the same color on Miss Dunlop's shoes." *Turn to 201.*

542

You watch Grayson as he levels his gun at Mortimer. Then Captain Leaf announces the rules to Mortimer and Snead, who stand ready. "He won't really fire,' you tell yourself. 'That's impossible!'

"I will say ready, and then count to five, gentlemen," Leaf announces. "You may fire at anytime after I begin to count, but you must fire before the count of five."

"Ready! One!" Mortimer's gun fires. "Two!...Three!"

Snead's pistol and Grayson's rifle crack simultaneously. Mortimer cries out in pain, falling to the ground. The women scream, and the men shout in consternation at the sight. You jump from your place and calling out, point to where Grayson was hidden. The solicitor turns and flees quickly through the woods as Watson, Colonel Dunlop and others run to where you stand. Quickly you explain what happened. Grayson's abandoned rifle and his flight confirm your story. "But why in God's name didn't you stop the bounder?" Dunlop roars. "What kind of a detective are you?"

"I was not sure what he intended," you explain, but your logic seems inadequate. The subsequent pursuit of Grayson proves fruitless. The criminal has escaped!

You are grateful to dine in Gunston that evening. You and Watson join Holmes at a small inn. As you outline the facts of the case, Mr. Holmes listens silently but with customary attention. "But why did he do it?" Watson demands, visibly shaken. "I don't understand."

• *If you checked Clue L and either Clue K or N, turn to 427.*

• *If you checked Clue K or N but not Clue L, turn to 318.*

• *Otherwise, turn to 354.*

As you turn to enter the dining room, the Colonel signals you to join him in his study for a moment. "What is the matter, sir?" you ask, as he closes the door behind him.

"Someone tried to force their way into the library last night," he says, obviously concerned. He clasps his hands in front of him, perhaps to keep them from trembling. "When Beach opened the house this morning, he found that the door from the hallway to the library had been unlocked, although the bolts were not touched. We may be fortunate that we still have the eagle. What do you think?"

You blush a little, then quickly explain your expedition of the night before. "So you see," you conclude, "there is nothing to worry about."

"Well, please be careful," the Colonel says, "I do not want my guests to know that I have brought a detective among them. But still," he adds with a nervous laugh, "it sounds as if you need a few more burglary lessons. You didn't know that locking a door is sometimes as difficult as unlocking it, did you? Now come to breakfast." The Colonel leads you to the dining room and begins to fill his plate with bacon and eggs. ***Turn to 309.***

After the meal, there is still some time before the exchange of shots, which is to take place at five minutes past noon. You remember that Watson brought the guns from the house himself. "You carried the guns, John," you say, probing a bit. "Have you checked them to see if they were loaded? It would be tragic if someone were actually shot today."

"No chance of that," he answers, laughing at the idea. "I cleaned both weapons before I took them from the gun room, and no one has touched them since. Foxx will load them with powder only, just before they are handed to Mortimer and Snead." Check Clue O. ***Turn to 381.***

545

You continue to examine the pistols. They are clean and empty, ready for use. You find nothing strange about them and to the relief of the Colonel, return them to their case. *Turn to 426.*

546

The steamer chest is filled with clothes. Evidently Snead does not believe in unpacking when he is spending only a few days in a house. You measure the chest to see that it has no hidden compartments. *Pick a number and add your Observation Bonus:*
• *If 2-6, turn to 547.*
• *If 7-12, turn to 550.*

547

You find nothing else in the chest and repack it with great care, making certain that you arrange it exactly as you found it. *Turn to 562.*

548

You try to examine the door, its locks, and the bolts at the top and bottom, hoping that you can prove whether or not someone has used this door recently. *Pick a number and add your Scholarship bonus:*
• *If 2-7, turn to 504.*
• *If 8-12, turn to 266.*

549

"It's an easy life to grow accustomed to," Harris replies, "and if you put all your skill and energy into your business, you may own such a house one day. Now me," he says with a practiced laugh, "I was not forced to find money in such a way. I was very fortunate. My uncle left me an income of four thousand a year two years ago, and I shall inherit more when my father passes away. I can do the things that I enjoy, unlike most, who must earn their living." *Check Deduction 6. Turn to 502.*

The last object you examine is a dirty handkerchief, crumpled in a corner at the bottom of the chest. When you pick it up, it feels heavy; you find that it is wrapped around three lead balls. The balls could fit the duelling pistols. You carefully return everything to its place in the chest, making sure it is arranged just as Snead left it. *Check Clue DD*. **Turn to 562**.

"There is one piece of evidence that points only toward Miss Dunlop," you comment. "The thief dropped the eagle into a chair in the library, a sign that the thief was not strong enough to carry the bird down the ladder. The only suspect who is not physically strong is Miss Dunlop."

"That is evidence," Holmes replies, "but it is not substantial proof. Surely that is not your only piece of evidence."

• *If you checked Clue EE*, **turn to 114**.

• *Otherwise*, **turn to 437**.

You recall that the prowler of two nights ago was interested in the pistols. 'I wonder if he did anything to them,' you think.

• *If you ask to examine the pistols*, **turn to 386**.

• *Otherwise*, **turn to 426**.

In spite of your nervousness, you manage to hit the target. The ladies are kind enough to clap. Then you continue to aim and fire as Redruth points to an even smaller target, then to a series of other objects — apples, cans, tree branches. Finally only four competitors remain: you, Watson, Grayson and Snead.

Redruth's newest target is very clever. He hangs apples from strings and starts them spinning. You must shoot while the apple is moving. **Pick a number** and add your Athletics bonus:

• *If 2-9*, **turn to 494**.

• *If 10-12*, **turn to 245**.

554

"I watched very carefully while the pistols were loaded," you say. "They had only powder in them when they were handed to the duellists. Therefore, Mr. Snead had to be the one who put a shot in his gun."

"A logical explanation," Holmes says, and you smile at his words. "It is unfortunate that you are so wrong." *Turn to 188.*

555

As you glance across the meadow, you see the breeze gently stirring the tall grass and bushes along its edge. Something looks out of place — but what? *Pick a number* and add your Observation bonus:
• If 2-9, *turn to 155.*
• If 10-12, *turn to 274.*

556

"I believe that the thief must have taken it upstairs and hidden it," you say, quite unsure. "There are corners up there where no one would look for it."

Holmes shakes his head almost before you finish speaking. "If you had searched the upper floors, as I did," he says, "you would know that the eagle is not hidden there."

"Then where is it, Holmes?" Watson asks in a testy voice. "Come to the library, and I shall show you," Holmes answers, leading the way. *Turn to 310.*

557

Using your mind, you recall some of the advice that Holmes gave in his monograph on the measurement of footprints. Searching your pockets, you find two items which will allow you to make an estimate of the footprint. First, you measure the length and width with a piece of string, then you press two pieces of paper over the print; the surrounding mud leaves an outline. You trace this outline onto dry pieces of paper.

Returning to the house, you and Watson explain what you discovered to Colonel Dunlop. In a shocked voice, he says: "But the rifle was one of mine. That means the gunman must be a guest, either Harris or Grayson! You see, the servants were occupied at the time of the shooting, and no outsider could steal a gun from the house." At your suggestion, the Colonel asks Beach to get one each of Harris's and Grayson's shoes and bring them to his study. You measure each of them by your methods. Grayson's shoe fits the mark on the paper perfectly and matches the string. You nod grimly, while the Colonel stares in shock. "So Grayson is the criminal," he says. "But why? He had no reason to shoot Mortimer. Tell me: why did he do it?" *Check Clue X.*

• *If you checked Clue L and Clue K or N,* **turn to 569.**
• *Otherwise,* **turn to 565.**

558

You glance towards the woods as Leaf calls: "Ready! One!" One pistol fires. "Two!...Three!" The other gun fires. Then, to your astonishment, you see a puff of smoke rise from the woods, where you had seen movement earlier. Mortimer cries out in pain! Is he shot? The women scream, and cries of panic issue from the other men. *Check Clue T.*

• *If you tell someone about the smoke,* **turn to 276.**
• *Otherwise,* **turn to 448.**

"I believe that someone shot Mortimer because they hated him," you say somewhat hesitantly. "Often, the target of the bullet is the intended victim."

"Perhaps," Holmes replies, staring at you with intense eyes, "but do you have any evidence indicating who hated Mortimer enough to shoot him?"

• *If you checked Deduction 11,* **turn to 430.**
• *Otherwise,* **turn to 488.**

560

The only item of note in the library that you did not examine closely earlier was the eagle. With no one around, you might be able to take a very close look at the way it is secured, and also learn how difficult it might be to snatch the golden bird.

• *If you try to look at the eagle,* **turn to 328.**
• *If you leave the library,* **turn to 595.**

561

"I would feel better if I remained here to keep watch," you say, and the Colonel is unable to change your mind. After leaving his study, you settle in the drawing room to continue reading the book which caught your attention earlier. *Check Decision 26.* **Pick a number** *and add your Observation bonus:*

• *If 2-5,* **turn to 126.**
• *If 6-12,* **turn to 390.**

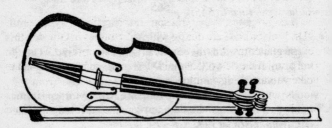

562

You stare at the steamer chest, for there is something odd about it, something that you should have noticed. *Pick a number* and add your Intuition Bonus:

- *If 2-7, turn to 107.*
- *If 8-12, turn to 286.*

563

Though you try to move quietly, the brush and grass seem to conspire against your efforts. You slow down, to let Grayson widen his lead, hoping that the noise you make will not alert him to your pursuit. Soon, you realize that you have let him get too far ahead. You have lost his trail! Unhappy at your failure, you return to the house and try to settle down with your book once more. What can he be up to? *Turn to 160.*

564

"But I know this of Grayson," you insist, not yielding an inch to Watson. "Before you met me in the library, he came in, talking with Jackson. Grayson noted the value of the eagle and spoke openly of his own need for money. Now such need does not automatically make a man a criminal, but it does provide a motive, wouldn't you agree?" Your cousin declines to reply. "I do not say that I suspect him," you continue, "but he cannot be dismissed from consideration." Watson shakes his head but does not argue the point. *Turn to 378.*

565

"I do not know why Grayson shot Mortimer," you admit. "Dr. Watson and I are dining with Mr. Holmes in Gunston this evening. Perhaps he will be able to suggest a motive." Though unhappy at the delay, Colonel Dunlop orders his coachman to take you and Watson into Guston.

As you enter the door of the Gunston Arms, you see Holmes talking with the barman; they appear to be drinking ale from tall mugs. *Turn to 394.*

566

Satisfied that you have carefully searched Snead's room, you return to the hall and turn towards Foxx's room. *Turn to 512*.

567

You look around the lower floor of the library, still trying to find signs of the thief or his actions. To one side of the fireplace, you spy the small door of a dumbwaiter in the wall. As you go over to examine it, the Colonel comments: "Surely you do not think the thief hid there, do you?"

"I merely want to search every possible corner of the room," you answer. "Mr. Holmes has often found key clues in the most absurd places." The Colonel nods and watches you as you work.

• *If you checked Clue C, turn to 141*.
• *Otherwise, turn to 383*.

568

Leaving the patch of mud, you return to the house to continue your investigation. *Turn to 196*.

569

"Money is the motive," you confidently tell Colonel Dunlop, "though it came in a round-about way. Grayson's business is known to be desperately short of capital."

"But what has that to do with Mortimer?" the Colonel demands, as if defending the solicitor.

"You see, Colonel, if Snead and Susan Mortimer marry, they will inherit a large sum of money which Grayson currently controls," you explain. "That money must be invested in Grayson's business. If he were forced to withdraw it to pay them, the loss would probably ruin him."

"But why shoot Mortimer, rather than Snead?"

"Grayson did not want to kill anybody," you continue, "but he knew that if Snead appeared to wound Mortimer, it would prevent the wedding. As Snead must leave the country soon, there would be little chance for a reconciliation. Thus, Grayson could maintain sole control of the funds for a long time to come." As you leave the house, you hear Colonel Dunlop instructing Beach to clear all of Grayson's things out of the house at once, before ordering the butler to bar the solicitor from re-entering Eagle Towers.

After brief congratulations, you and Watson drive into Gunston, to dine with Holmes at the Gunston Inn. The great detective listens carefully as you explain the case, then smiles. "You have done very well," he admits, tamping his pipe tobacco, "to solve so complicated an affair so quickly. To my mind, you took advantage of every important clue that came your way."

You savor the compliment, and as Holmes begins to explain how he solved the jewel thefts, you sit back and dream a little, wondering what kind of case you will investigate next. Will it be an attempted murder? A kidnapping? Or worse? The End

570

"In addition to deducing that your niece was the only person who could have run through the mud," you continue, "I examined her shoes and found some of the mud on them, which confirms my deduction." *Turn to 201*.

571

"For how long have you been in England?" you ask Snead.

"For about two months, or thereabouts," he replies, nibbling a sandwich. "I'm in the shipping business in Canada, and I am here to make some credit arrangements which can only be made in person. I had intended to stay for only a few weeks, but other matters lengthened the visit," he says, smiling at Susan Mortimer, who laughs gaily with him.

• *If you ask him more about his business, turn to 370.*
• *Otherwise, turn to 385.*

Holmes listens to your vague explanation of the motive, then shakes his head. "You have not established a motive," he says. "You must do better in future investigations. It is not enough to be right — you must also prove that you are right." *Turn to 303.*

573

"John," you inquire, puzzled, "How could there have been a ball in that gun? It was loaded only with powder. You and I both know that."

"We cannot be certain," answers Dr. Watson. "We did not watch the loading of the guns at close range. No one saw the need. And if we had watched, it would have been easy for someone casually handling the guns to drop a ball in with a little sleight of hand." *Turn to 103.*

574

"It's an easy life to grow used to," Harris replies, displaying a broad smile. He is a handsome fellow. "I would press my advantages if I were you, sir, and perhaps you shall one day have such a house." He shifts the conversation into other channels, but from his talk of the many weeks that he has spent at country houses, you discern that he does not find it necessary to earn a living. *Turn to 502.*

575

You walk down the hall and stop outside Miss Dunlop's door. Recalling the evidence you have assembled, you wonder: 'should I search her room, or can I spare the pleasant young lady that indignity?'

• *If you search the room, turn to 134.*
• *Otherwise, turn to 111.*

576

"I have been thinking the matter over," you say, "and I think that the eagle must be hidden behind the books in the library. The thief would not have dared to take it further until things settled down a little." Although he laughs at the idea, the Colonel agrees to go down to the library with you. The group looks behind and around all the books that could be reached without a ladder. The eagle is not there. *Turn to 310.*

577

Deeply dejected, you watch the stream wash away the footmark. Your efforts to use a straight treelimb and your hands to measure the clue failed. You have lost one of the strongest clues to come your way since the shot was fired; Holmes would have found some way to measure that footprint! Disgusted with yourself, you return to the house. *Turn to 525.*

578

Inside your room, you sit back in a comfortable chair and begin to read Holmes' monograph on the different kinds of tobacco ash. As you read, you hear some disturbance and loud voices from downstairs. Rising, you go downstairs and see the butler and a groom escorting a roughly-dressed man out the front door. Watson meets you halfway up the stairs. "Ah, there you are, cousin," he says in greeting, leading you back up to your room. "You missed the excitement of the evening."

"Something to do with the eagle?" you ask anxiously.

"Oh no, not at all," Watson answers. "But young Mortimer caught a poacher, a well- known local fellow named Badger Phillips. Mortimer was out for a walk and caught the rascal trying to snare some birds."

"What did the Colonel do?" you ask.

"Not much," Watson answers, "at least, not much for the moment. He told the fellow to come before him Tuesday for judgment." *Turn to 338.*

You ask the Colonel for a word in the solitude of his study. "I have finished my investigation," you announce.

"Who is the culprit?" Dunlop demands. A facial twitch betrays the Colonel's outward calm.

"I would rather wait a moment more before I make an accusation," you answer. "Doctor Watson and I will dine with Mr. Holmes in Gunston this evening. I should like to go into town now and ask him to review my deductions before I point a finger at anyone."

The Colonel stares at you in amazement. "Sherlock Holmes is in Gunston?" he asks. "Then I shall send the coach for him at once! Why should I depend upon you when I can have the opinion of the greatest detective in the world?" He calls for Beach, gives instructions, and soon the coach is racing towards Gunston to pick up Holmes.

While you wait, hiding your embarassment, you join the others in the drawing room. Immediately Captain Leaf joins you and Watson, launching into a story about an odd wedding he witnessed in India. This story leads him to recap the day's events, and he comments: "It certainly is odd to see a re-enactment of the duel apparently prevent a wedding between Snead and Mortimer, eh?" He then chuckles as though it reminded him of another of his collection of tales.

- *If you ask Leaf what he meant, **turn to 293**.*
- *Otherwise, **turn to 403**.*

You learn very little from your conversation with Harris. He turns the talk back to the events of the weekend, mentioning with special relish the shooting contest scheduled for the morrow. "You had best take cover when Robert is shooting," Miss Dunlop adds. "The safest place for all is behind the target," she jests. As he frowns at her sally, she drags him off to the serving table heavily laden with cakes and sandwiches. ***Turn to 590.***

581

"I found balls to fit the duelling pistols hidden in Mr. Snead's trunk," you say. "It seems logical that the man who had the shot loaded the gun."

"It is logical," Holmes says, "but it is not correct. Anyone could have slipped those balls into the trunk, for Snead leaves the key in the lock." *Turn to 188.*

582

As you chat with Robert Snead and Miss Mortimer, you try to consider just what to ask him: what question would be most provocative yet not too forward?
• *If you ask when and why he first came to England, turn to 571.*
• *Otherwise, turn to 385.*

583

"I have no solid evidence," you admit, "but the most obvious person to accuse is the man with the gun in his hand. No one knew which gun would go to which man."

"There is logic in your explanation," Holmes admits, "but you are wrong." Your momentary sensation of satisfaction disappears. *Turn to 188.*

584

Employing the methods Holmes has taught you, you see that Grayson broke a path through some bushes, and you soon pick up his trail. You follow the solicitor carefully. If you allow Grayson to get too big a lead, you will lose track of him. However, if you follow too closely, he will hear you, and an unpleasant incident might follow. You try to move quietly enough to stay quite near him. *Pick a number and add your Artifice bonus:*
• *If 2-8, turn to 563.*
• *If 9-12, turn to 531.*

Having enjoyed a restful night's sleep, you arise when the footman brings tea. You and Watson dress quickly and go down to breakfast. *Turn to 599.*

586

You watch Grayson enter the shadowy woods and wonder vaguely whether his trip to town might be less than legitimate. As soon as he is out of sight, you hurry to follow him. When you enter the woods, the trees have already hidden him, and you quickly look for signs of his path. *Pick a number and add your Observation bonus:*

• *If 2-8, turn to 244.*
• *If 9-12, turn to 584.*

587

You are certain that Foxx did nothing unusual to the guns, although he might have slipped a ball into one gun without your seeing it.

Then you relax a bit; there is no reason for Foxx to do anything unusual to the pistols — even if he were culpable, he could not be certain which gun would be given to which man. *Check Clue R. Turn to 320.*

588

"The wound proves that someone else shot Mortimer," you say. "A shot from where Snead stood could not scrape the back of Mortimer's neck. The slug would have been forced to take an elliptical course, of all things!"

"Very good," Holmes says, as the others consider your comment and nod in agreement. "I was amused that no one had recognized that Snead could not possibly have wounded Mortimer." *Turn to 536.*

589

The Colonel almost hugs the heavy eagle to his chest. Quickly he returns to his study, and with your asistance, locks the eagle in the safe. "Before anything else happens to it," the Colonel notes. *Turn to 115.*

590

As you turn from the receding Harris and Miss Dunlop, the Colonel rejoins you. He leads and introduces you to Dr. Cunningham, a gossipy old man who ties up Watson with professional talk for several long minutes. Breaking loose from Dr. Cunningham, you meet Lieutenant John Mortimer, his sister Susan, and a fellow named Robert Snead. The Mortimer siblings are tall, with dark brown hair and vivid eyes. While Miss Mortimer seems as lively as Miss Dunlop, her brother is much more serious. Snead is a bit of a puzzle to you, even after you are told that he is to marry Miss Mortimer shortly. A man of medium height — indeed, he is not much taller than his fiance — with straight, black hair Snead seems a friendly, rather simple fellow, and his accent tells you he is a Canadian. To you, he appears to be a fish out of water. Why is he here?

• *If you ask Snead,* **turn to 262.**
• *Otherwise,* **turn to 436.**

591

Desperately you bring to mind evidence supporting your statement.

• *If you checked Clue S,* **turn to 522.**
• *Otherwise,* **turn to 214.**

592

"Badger Phillips, the poacher, shot Mortimer," you say. "His anger at Mortimer provides a motive, and a poacher would probably be a good shot."

"There are some grounds for your accusation," Holmes admits, "but there is no solid evidence to support it. If Phillips held a grudge against Mortimer, he would try to thrash him rather than attempt to murder him. The crime is far out of proportion to the motive." **Turn to 225.**

593

"You have no proof at all," Holmes says, quite disappointed by your failure. "You must have evidence, even if you have established a powerful motive."

- *If you want to investigate again,* **turn to the Prologue.**
- *If you want to hear Holmes' explanation,* **turn to 290.**
- *If you want to explain the motive,* **turn to 298.**

594

"When Mr. Grayson left for Gunston," you say, "I decided to follow him. I did not follow him all the way, but I saw him leave the path to town and come back through the woods toward the house. That would place him in the woods overlooking the duelling grounds, at the right time. He had no reason for such suspicious behavior, unless he was the hidden marksman."

"A very strong piece of evidence," Holmes says. "It is unfortunate that you did not follow him all the way. Then you might have been able to prevent the shooting. Your proof will be impressive if you can offer a motive for the shooting." You consider Holmes' question.

- *If you checked Clue L and either Clue K or N,* **turn to 301.**
- *If you checked Clue L,* **turn to 299.**
- *Otherwise,* **turn to 572.**

595

Having completed your examination of the library, you quietly slip out the portal. You carefully close the gates and secure the chain and padlock. No one will know that you were in the library. **Turn to 393.**

596

As Snead's shot echoes across the clearing, you hear a cry of pain from Mortimer, an exclamation quickly drowned by the screams of the women and the shocked voices of the other men. You look see to see Mortimer on the ground, one hand clutching his neck, blood visible from where you stand. **Turn to 159.**

"Will anything unusual happen when Snead marries Susan Mortimer?" Leaf repeats. "They will inherit a great deal of money that they do not know about. Is that unusual?"

"How can that be?" you ask in astonishment.

"Old Colonel Murphy, who commanded the battery at Waterloo, left his estate to the first Snead and Mortimer to marry," Leaf patiently explains. "The money has been building in trust for many years, and rather rapidly of late, I think. That sharp fellow Grayson has been the trustee." You talk with Leaf for a moment longer, then drift away as others enter, hunting the brandy decanter. *Check Clue L.* **Turn to 140.**

598

You walk slowly back to the house, contemplating the clues you have gathered, and tell the Colonel that you have something important to discuss with him and his niece.

"What is so important?" the Colonel asks, a bit exasperated. "Have you identified the thief?"

You look at Ellen and for a moment, pity her; she is shaking with fear. But you owe the Colonel an honest answer.

"Your niece Ellen stole the eagle," you say, unable to raise your eyes from the ground.

"What?" the Colonel roars, searching for a club or a cane to thrash you with. "What kind of an idiotic notion have you gotten into your head —"

Soon, his roar subsides, for Ellen falls into a chair and sobs miserably. "I traced her movements and discovered her muddy footprints," you say, not at all pleased in spite of your clever work. The Colonel tries to comfort her, stroking her hair and speaking gently, asking her why she would do such a thing.

"Oh, Uncle Alex!" the young woman finally says, whimpering. "It was because of that horrible shooting, and what happened after. I knew that Thomas Snead could not possibly have been responsible for shooting Mortimer, and when the Mortimers threatened to prohibit the marriage, I had to do something! Snead said he was going to leave, and if he had done so, he never would have had a chance to be reconciled with Susan."

"But what has that to do with the eagle?" the Colonel asks, flustered.

"I knew that you would not allow anyone to leave if the eagle disappeared," she says, "and I hoped the delay would allow a reconciliation, once the first shock of the shooting had passed." The Colonel frowns at her. *Check Deduction 23*.
• *If you checked Decision 21*, **turn to 110**.
• *Otherwise*, **turn to 421**.

599

Once more you enjoy a filling country breakfast, the sort to keep a man going for the entire day, if necessary. Everyone has come down from their rooms, and excited talk about the re-creation of the duel fills the air. You notice Snead and Mortimer teasing each other, a slight edge apparent in their comments.

An odd thought strikes you; could something could go wrong with the duel? The re-creation seems to have been arranged very carefully. As you sip tea, you study the others. *Pick a number* and add your *Observation bonus*:
• *If 2-5*, **turn to 447**.
• *If 6-12*, **turn to 116**.

"I doubt that I have ever seen a more beautiful piece of work than that golden eagle," you say casually.

Captain Leaf smiles at the opening. "You will never see the like again," he answers. "Wellington, the Iron Duke, gave the Yorkshire Lights the right to add an eagle to our battery honours."

"Indeed!" you exclaim, humoring the captain.

He goes on before you can say more. "It was after the Battle of Vittoria, at the end of the campaign in Spain. At Vittoria, the Yorkshires made a spectacular record. Our guns had been bogged down by the loss of our horses, and we were unable to use them to hurry the departure of the fleeing frogs. But the commander was a true soldier; he joined his men to a battalion of Highlanders. Together they shattered a French Battalion and captured its eagle. The Highlanders kept the French Eagle but the Duke allowed our men to make a replica."

"Nothing else in England like it, nothing outside the Tower," Leaf brags, his eyes glistening at the memory. "When the French fled the field at Vittoria, their baggage train bogged down, and our men got into it. The French had all the plunder that they had stolen from Spain over many years, and our boys seized most of it. But the officers of the Yorkshire Lights didn't keep it for themselves; believe it or not, each officer contributed what his men had captured to be made into the eagle. And when they saw the result, they all agreed that it was well worth the cost." The captain keeps on with his history, drowning your every attempt to turn the conversation toward a different path. Finally, Watson manages to interrupt and rescue you. *Turn to 263.*

As you stare at the dumbwaiter ropes, you realize that something is odd. Someone has twisted some wire around the rope. No wonder it is impossible to move the thing. Why would anyone do such a thing?

• *If you free the ropes and lower the dumbwaiter,*
 turn to 316.
• *If you would rather wait before freeing the ropes,*
 turn to 466.

"I recall something of Grayson, now," you say slowly. "I had forgotten, because he did not speak of it himself. If I am not mistaken, he is the managing director of one of the new railroads now under construction, the Whitby and York. I remember reading in the newspapers that while the project will be very successful if finished, its finances are stretched to the limit now, and the railroad's backers have not been able to attract further investment. The value of the eagle might make the difference between success and failure in this vast enterprise."

"Highly unlikely," Watson replies, sniffing in distaste, "for a gentleman does not rob his host to finance a railroad. It's not done!" *Check Clue N.* **Turn to 378.**

603

"I subscribe to Holmes' view," you answer. "Almost anyone can be a legitimate suspect, especially if one notes something unusual in their actions. Regarding Grayson, for example: did you know that he arranged to be invited here? Otherwise, he should not be among us."

"Well," Watson says, a gleam in his eye, "if you had the chance to cadge an invitation to Colonel Dunlop's table, would you decline the opportunity? I have seldom enjoyed so pleasant a weekend."
- *If you checked Clue K,* **turn to 564.**
- *Otherwise,* **turn to 261.**

604

"Do you know why Grayson shot Mortimer?" Holmes asks. "The evidence you offer is not overwhelming; thus, you must demonstrate a motive to prove your case." You consider your evidence.
- *If you checked Clue L and either Clue K or N,*
  turn to 301.
- *If you checked Clue L,* **turn to 299.**
- *Otherwise,* **turn to 572.**

Wanted!

Solo Gamebook Writers!

I.C.E. is looking for a few good writers in three lines of **SOLO ADVENTURES:** *Sherlock Holmes Solo Mysteries™*, *Narnia Solo Games™*, and *Middle-earth Quest Gamebooks™*. If you meet the following requirements, send us a two-page plot synopsis or project idea along with your resume.

• Familiarity with Questbooks and/or Roleplaying games.

• Ability to write well and meet deadlines.

• Access to a computer.

• Willingness to work as a team player.

Respond with a SASE to:

    Managing Gamebook Editor

    Iron Crown Enterprises

    P.O. Box 1605

    Charlottesville, VA 22902

WE NEED YOUR FEEDBACK!

PLEASE HELP US DO A BETTER JOB ON FUTURE BOOKS BY ANSWERING SOME OR ALL OF THE FOLLOWING QUESTIONS & SENDING YOUR REPLIES TO I.C.E.:

I purchased this book at _____ _____(name of store).

The name of this book is _____ _____.

I am (male/female) _____, and _____ years of age. I am in the _____ grade in school.

I live in a (small, medium, large) _____ town/city.

My favorite magazine is _____.

I heard about this gamebook through _____ _____ (a friend, a family member, an advertisement, other _____).

The one thing I like the *most* about this Sherlock Holmes Solo Mystery is _____ _____ _____ .

The one thing I like the *least* about this Sherlock Holmes Solo Mystery is _____ _____ _____

Send all feedback replies to:

IRON CROWN ENTERPRISES
P.O. BOX 1605, DEPT., SH
CHARLOTTESVILLE, VA. 22902

Rolemaster ™

I.C.E.'s advanced Fantasy Role Playing Game
system. ROLEMASTER is a complete set of
the most advanced, realistic, and sophisticated
rules available. The flexibility of the system
allows it to be used wholly or in part.
ROLEMASTER's component parts include:
CHARACTER LAW & CAMPAIGN LAW,
ARMS LAW & CLAW LAW, and SPELL
LAW. Each of these can be used separately to
improve the realism of most major FRP
systems! Now you can add detail to your
fantasy gaming without sacrificing playability!
ROLEMASTER....a cut above the rest!

Produced & Distributed by
IRON CROWN
ENTERPRISES INC.
P.O. Box 1605
Charlottesville, VA 22902

MIDDLE-EARTH ROLE PLAYING™

MIDDLE-EARTH ROLE PLAYING (MERP) is a Fantasy Role Playing Game system perfect for novices as well as experienced gamers! Based on THE HOBBIT and THE LORD OF THE RINGS, MERP provides the structure and framework for role playing in the greatest fantasy setting of all time....J.R.R. Tolkien's Middle-earth! MERP is well supported by a wide variety of game aids, Campaign Modules, Adventure Supplements, and Ready-to-Run Adventures. MIDDLE-EARTH ROLE PLAYING....a world apart!

Produced & Distributed by
IRON CROWN
ENTERPRISES INC.
P.O. Box 1605
Charlottesville, VA 22902

RANDOM NUMBER TABLE

6	11	8	9	7	5	6	9	8	5	7	3
7	4	10	6	3	12	7	2	10	8	4	11
9	6	5	7	4	8	5	6	9	7	10	8
8	5	7	3	6	11	8	9	7	5	6	9
10	8	4	11	7	4	10	6	3	12	7	2
9	7	10	8	9	6	5	7	4	8	5	6
7	5	6	9	8	5	7	3	6	11	8	9
3	12	7	2	10	8	4	11	7	4	10	6
4	8	5	6	9	7	10	8	9	6	5	7
6	11	8	9	7	5	6	9	8	5	7	3
7	4	10	6	3	12	7	2	10	8	4	11
9	6	5	7	4	8	5	6	9	7	10	8
8	5	7	3	6	11	8	9	7	5	6	9
10	8	4	11	7	4	10	6	3	12	7	2
9	7	10	8	9	6	5	7	4	8	5	6